He wanted Cami

The thought surprised him. Why did he care?

But he'd seen the pleasure in her eyes as she'd looked at her reflection. The yearning. Her life was a wreck right now. She deserved something that would make her smile.

"I'll take it. Don't tell Camille. I want it to be a surprise," he told the saleswoman, credit card in hand. After she rang it up and placed it in a bag, he went out and hid it behind the seat in his truck, smiling when he thought of how happy Camille would be with his gift.

When Jericho returned to the shop, he saw Camille and his jaw dropped. She looked like every man's dream in a fitted blue-green top and a pair of matching shorts that hit her midthigh, showcasing her toned legs. She'd exchanged her pumps for green flat sandals. Even without a speck of makeup, she was drop-dead gorgeous. And she was more relaxed than she'd been since she arrived.

His heart, which he'd believed had died a year ago, jumped as if being recharged like a dead battery.

"I'm ready."

* * *

SWEET BRIAR SWEETHEARTS:
There's something about Sweet Briar...

Dear Reader,

I love romantic stories. I enjoy hearing about people who fell in love at first sight. It's so amazing when two people know in an instant that they've met *the one*. Then there are the couples who were friends and whose love grew over time. One minute they were pals and the next they were in love, and neither of them is sure when or how it happened. And there are the couples who traveled long and difficult roads and against all odds reached their happy ending. These couples support my belief that some people are fated to be together.

Jericho Jones (whom we met in *The Waitress's Secret*) and Camille Parker don't seem destined to fall in love. Not only are their lives totally different—she's a rising star in a Wall Street firm and he's a rancher in North Carolina—they hate each other.

When Camille's life is in danger, she heads to the one place no one will look for her, the Double J Ranch. After losing his wife and unborn child without warning, Jericho has become a recluse. He barely tolerates visits from old friends, so he definitely isn't happy when Camille shows up on his doorstep. Still, she was his late wife's former best friend. His wife had loved Camille, so he can't turn her away.

As the two spend time together, they travel the long path toward their happy ending. The road is rocky and has many twists and turns, but the happiness waiting at the end makes it all worthwhile.

I love hearing from my readers. Please visit my website, kathydouglassbooks.com. You can drop me an email or join my mailing list. I'm also on Facebook at Author Kathy Douglass.

Happy reading!

Kathy

The Rancher
and the City Girl

———

Kathy Douglass

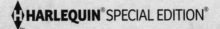

HARLEQUIN® SPECIAL EDITION®

ISBN-13: 978-1-335-46552-8

The Rancher and the City Girl

HARLEQUIN®
www.Harlequin.com

Printed in U.S.A.

Kathy Douglass came by her love of reading naturally—both of her parents were readers. She would finish one book and pick up another. Then she attended law school and traded romances for legal opinions.

After the birth of her two children, her love of reading turned into a love of writing. Kathy now spends her days writing the small-town contemporary novels she enjoys reading.

Books by Kathy Douglass

Harlequin Special Edition

Sweet Briar Sweethearts

How to Steal the Lawman's Heart
The Waitress's Secret
The Rancher and the City Girl

This book is dedicated with love to my husband and sons. Thanks for filling my life with love and joy.

Chapter One

Go somewhere no one will look for you. The words of warning echoed through Camille Parker's head as she sped down the rapidly darkening country road. It curved suddenly, and she almost lost control of the car. Cursing under her breath, she eased up on the accelerator and jerked the wheel, steering back onto the asphalt. They wouldn't have to kill her if she did it herself.

Slowing, she began looking for a mailbox. She had to be close by now. Finally she spotted a driveway flanked by two large trees. She stopped next to the mailbox, hoping to find a name and not just the street number. Luckily, she made out "Jericho and Jeanette Jones" in red letters on the metal box. Despite her anxiety, her heart squeezed at the sight of her former friend's name. How she had missed Jeanette. She always would.

Camille knew no one had followed her from New

York, yet she still checked her rearview mirror. Convinced that she was alone on the isolated lane, she turned into the long, winding crushed-rock driveway, driving as fast as she dared. She didn't want to lose control of the car again when she was this close to safety.

And what if Jericho didn't let her in? He hated her. And she hated him. She'd never used the term "sworn enemies" before, but it described their relationship more accurately than other words could.

Not only had he convinced Jeanette to break off her engagement to Camille's brother and marry him instead, he'd brought Jeanette out here to the middle of nowhere and let her die. Camille's eyes filled with tears as she recalled finding out about Jeanette's death in the obituary section of their high school's alumni newsletter. Just one more reason to hate Jericho.

The two-story house appeared around a bend, and she slowed the car, stopping as close to the building as possible. She opened the door and heaved a heavy sigh. Her heart beat hard against the walls of her chest as doubt once more assaulted her.

What if he didn't take her in?

She shoved aside that worry and tried again to silence the fear that had gripped her since she'd overheard her boss, Donald Wilcox, instructing someone to get rid of her and make it look like an accident. When she'd reached out in a panic to Rafael Delgado, her contact with the FBI, she discovered he was comatose after being in a car accident. That was when she'd run. At this point, she didn't know whom she could trust. That's why she needed to disappear for a while.

She couldn't go to her parents or her brother in Chicago. No doubt that would be the first place the killers would look. And they could easily discover the identities of the friends she'd made in New York, many of whom worked at the Wall Street firm with her, and those she'd left behind in Chicago. So their homes were off-limits, as well. She wouldn't put her family or friends at risk by seeking refuge with them. She had to go somewhere no one knew about or would ever think to look for her.

The Double J Ranch was just such a place. She and Jericho hadn't spoken civil words to each other in more than five years. More important, she hadn't spoken about him to anyone at the financial firm where she worked. No one in the New York banking circles would ever connect her to a horse rancher in North Carolina. The nearest town, Sweet Briar, was located almost an hour away on the ocean, so the ranch had the added bonus of being isolated. She'd be safe here. If he'd let her stay.

Her stomach seized as she considered the possibility that he might slam the door in her face. She couldn't let that happen. He was her last—no, her only—hope.

She couldn't risk using her credit cards or accessing her bank accounts once she'd left New York because even she knew she could be found that way. She'd been so rattled she hadn't given a thought to stopping at an ATM until she was well on her way to North Carolina. Then it was too late. After paying cash for her hotel room last night, she had only the $300 she always kept in her purse. Who would have thought she'd need to use her emergency funds in an actual emergency and not one that involved shopping? And who knew how long she would need to make this money last?

Grabbing her purse, she jumped from the car, then

raced up the short flight of stairs. She rang the door-bell several times, and a dog began barking. She heard scratching against the door as the barking grew louder and then stopped. She waited but heard no other sound. The urge to pound on the door nearly overcame her, but she pressed the doorbell for several long seconds instead. The barking started up again, but that's all she heard.

She didn't know anything about ranching. Would Jericho be in the house now, or out in the barn? Was the barn near the house? And what if he wasn't here at all?

She hadn't called to let him know she was coming. She couldn't. She didn't know his phone number. Not only that, she'd smashed and then discarded her cell phone, scattering the pieces along several New York streets so she couldn't be traced. That might have been overkill, but she'd rather be safe than sorry. She'd never had people trying to kill her before, so the only thing she knew to do was what she'd seen in movies.

She raised a fist to pound on the door, but it was suddenly wrenched open. She lost her balance and fell against the man inside. He steadied her but not before she got a whiff of his masculine scent. Despite the terror that had been nipping at her heels for a day and a half, some tiny part of her was aware of just how good he smelled. The scent of pine and leather mixed in with a hint of soap clung to his skin. More than that, he smelled of safety and security. Like home.

He set her away from him none too gently, and she banished the ridiculous thought from her mind before it could take root. Telling herself to buck up, she raised her head and looked into deep brown eyes. Shock flashed in them briefly before being replaced by anger and hatred, finally landing on ice.

"What are you doing here?"

Jericho's deep voice was even colder than his eyes. No surprise there.

"I said, why are you here?" His hard voice cut through her musings, bringing her fear to the fore.

"I need somewhere to stay."

He leaned in closer, and she realized that although her lips had moved, her voice had been a mere squeak. She cleared her throat and tried again. "I need somewhere to stay."

His eyes narrowed and he backed away. She wasn't sure whether he was inviting her in or planning to close the door in her face. Moving quickly, she stepped inside. A black Lab sat on its haunches several feet away, its tail thumping against the floor.

"Why?" He shook his head. "Never mind why. I don't care. I'm just surprised you believe you're going to stay here with me. As I recall you think this ranch is a worn-down piece of dirt in the middle of nowhere. And I'm just a farmer looking to hook up with a rich woman to support me. Those are your words, aren't they?"

Camille cringed but didn't look away from the fury in his eyes. She'd said those very words five years ago when Jeanette had confided she was ending her engagement to Camille's brother and running off to Las Vegas with Jericho. Amazingly, he had quoted her verbatim.

He stepped around her and grabbed the doorknob. Unless she spoke fast and explained her predicament, she'd be on the other side of that door with nowhere to go before another minute passed. Three hundred dollars wouldn't last long.

She put a hand on his arm. He had to listen to her. A hot jolt of electricity shot through her, and she yanked her hand away before her fingers were singed. What in the world was that? "Please. You have to let me stay here." She heard the rising hysteria in her voice and clamped down on it. She'd never convince him if she lost her head.

"I don't have to do anything."

His hand twisted the knob.

"Please, Jericho. Don't send me away. You're the only person I can turn to. People are trying to kill me. If they find me, I'm dead."

Someone was trying to kill her? Right. Surely she could do better than that. After all, this was the same woman who'd bribed her way into his Chicago hotel room barely an hour before he was set to fly to Las Vegas and marry Jeanette. He'd never forget how he'd emerged from the shower to find Camille sprawled across his bed wearing a sexy little nothing. He didn't know what game she'd been playing, but he hadn't been interested. He'd never told Jeanette what Camille had done. He couldn't hurt Jeanette that way. She'd gone to her grave naively believing Camille Parker was worthy of her friendship. He knew better.

"Nice try, Camille. But I'm not buying it. Go play your games with someone else."

"It's not a game," she screeched, wild-eyed. "If you make me leave, they'll kill me."

Jericho released the knob and took a closer look at the woman in front of him. The haughty expression she'd worn like other women wore a favorite lipstick was missing. Now, rather than curling her lips in disdain, she mercilessly nibbled away at them.

Not caring that it was rude, he let his eyes travel over her body. Tall and thin, she was cover-girl beautiful. The few times he'd seen her, she'd been perfectly coifed and her clothes impeccable. Now her shoulder-length hair looked a mess. The curls were tangled as if she had run her fingers through them over and over. The scarf that had held her locks away from her face was edging toward the back of her head. Her clothes were wrinkled, as if she'd slept in them. There was a frantic expression on her face, and she looked about ready to jump out of her skin.

Could someone really be trying to kill her? And if that was true, what did it have to do with him? "What's going on?"

Camille jumped, and he realized he'd yelled his question. Her chest rose and fell as she inhaled deeply. She lifted a shaky hand and ran it through her hair, then adjusted her scarf. The smile she gave him was so forced he wondered why she bothered. "It's a long story."

"Just cut to the chase. I don't have time to waste with meaningless details. And if the situation is as dire as you claim, you don't either."

"Right." She compressed her lips, then looked him dead in the eyes. "I told you. Someone is trying to kill me."

"But why come here? As I recall they have police in Chicago."

"New York City. I moved to New York eight months ago to start a new job."

"Okay. Not that it makes a difference. They have police there, too."

"I can't go to them. I don't know who I can trust. I know there's at least one person in the government involved. Maybe the police are, too. I just can't risk it."

Even without the details, this story was too convoluted to hear all the way through while standing in the hallway, not to mention that she was too edgy for his liking and he needed some space from her. So he gestured for her to proceed into his living room.

Her eyes widened in surprise before she let out a breath of what was clearly relief and stumbled ahead of him. She looked around uncertainly before he nodded and pointed toward the chairs before the unlit fireplace. He and Jeanette had spent many winter evenings sitting before a roaring fire. He hadn't lit it once since her death. He'd avoided this room, coming in only to clean on rare occasions because the memories were unbearable. Still he'd rather live with the discomfort than let Camille intrude farther into his home.

"Would you like a drink?" he asked automatically, then wanted to bite his tongue. This wasn't a social call. And he definitely didn't want to prolong her stay.

"No thanks," she said and sank into a chair. The dog immediately put his head on her lap.

"Shadow, heel."

Shadow whined, then raced from the room. A minute later he returned carrying a chew toy that he dropped at Jericho's feet. Jericho ignored the rubber bone and walked past what Jeanette had referred to as his chair, choosing instead to lean against the fireplace mantel.

"I work for a financial institution. An investment banking firm. I'm very good at what I do."

He nodded and gestured for her to get on with her story. He didn't have all night to listen to her.

"A few months ago I was working on one of my boss's accounts and I noticed something was off with the numbers. He was out of the office and I was answering a client's questions. Anyway, the numbers weren't adding up. I did a little digging and discovered that one of the vice presidents was massaging the numbers. He was juggling accounts in a way that's illegal. Money would appear and disappear. I knew something was fishy. I should have just quit, but I couldn't turn a blind eye. I dug a little deeper and discovered he was laundering money. I reported it to the government. The FBI agent I was working with needed more information to open a case, so I kept looking until I found it."

She wrung her hands and looked around the room. He had a suspicion she wasn't seeing the furniture Jeanette had so lovingly chosen, or the spectacular artwork she had purchased. No, the faraway look in her eyes let him know she was seeing something else entirely.

"Yesterday afternoon I was on my way to a meeting. I needed a pen, so I stepped into the supply closet to grab one. I overheard my boss talking with someone and heard my name. He told them to kill me and make it look like an accident." She shivered and wrapped her arms around her waist. "I waited until they were gone and got out of there. I knew I couldn't go home."

"Are you sure about what you heard? This sounds a little far-fetched to me."

"I know what I heard."

"Your imagination—"

"I'm not imagining anything." Her voice rose and her eyes flashed. "I know what I heard. I know they want to kill me. If I die, the case dies with me."

He closed his eyes. She could be lying, but he couldn't imagine why she would bother. And she really did seem scared. Nobody could be that good an actress. But then, she had pretended to be Jeanette's friend, so maybe she did possess the skill. Still, he couldn't figure out why she would show up out of the blue. She didn't stand to gain anything by coming to him.

"I'm sorry for bringing trouble to your door, but I didn't know what else to do. I couldn't go to my parents' home. That's the first place they'll look. Same with Rodney and my friends. No one in New York knows a thing about you, so they won't look here."

"What about that agent you mentioned? The guy you told about this."

"I called his office. They told me he'd been in a car accident. That's pretty coincidental, don't you think?"

"People have accidents all the time, Camille." Still a sense of unease crept up his spine, which was a shock in itself, given the fact that he hadn't felt anything since Jeanette's death. Jericho paced the room for several minutes, trying to make sense of what he'd heard. It was just crazy enough to be true. She could be in danger.

But so what? She wasn't his problem. She wasn't his friend. Truth was, he'd categorize her as an enemy if he'd bothered to think of her, which he hadn't. Still…

"We haven't spoken in five years. You and your family disowned Jeanette simply because she fell in love with me. And now you expect me to step in and save you?"

Her shoulders sagged and her head dropped to her chest. After a few seconds she nodded, squared her shoulders, grabbed her purse and stood. "I understand. Sorry for bothering you." She headed for the door.

He should let her go. After the way she had treated Jeanette it was no more than she deserved. He was under no obligation to help her. Surely there had to be someone else she could turn to. Except…she had come to him. Despite how much he detested her, he knew Jeanette had loved her like a sister. She'd loved the entire Parker family. And at one time they'd loved her. Jeanette had never given up hope that one day they would reconcile and become friends again.

Jeanette and Camille had grown up together. When Jeanette's parents were killed in a plane crash when she was seventeen, the Parkers had taken her in. So no matter how much he loathed Camille, even if he would have been happy to never see her again in this life or the next, he would help her because her family had helped Jeanette.

"Wait."

She turned and looked at him. If he'd seen even a hint of triumph in her expression he would have kicked her out without the slightest remorse. Instead her hazel eyes revealed trepidation and a sliver of hope. He knew then that allowing her to stay was the right thing to do. He could never send a woman into danger, no matter how much he hated her. If there was a way he could keep her safe, he had to do it.

"You can stay."

Her knees wobbled, and she reached for the door. Unfortunately, she was too far away to grab it. He rushed forward and caught her as she collapsed, sweeping her into his arms. Her gentle scent wafted in the air and wrapped around him. Some random part of his brain noticed how well she fit in his arms, but he quickly banished the unwelcome thought.

"I'm okay. I can walk," she said in a small voice that belied her words. "It was just a little weakness, you know, from all the nerves. I've been so scared."

He ignored her protests and kept her in his arms until he reached the sofa, where he gently eased her onto the cushions. "When was the last time you ate?"

Her brow wrinkled, and she closed her eyes. "I'm not sure."

No doubt she was running on adrenaline coupled with a good dose of fear. Now that she was safe, her strength was gone. "Here's an easier question. When was the last time you slept?"

She laughed mirthlessly. "I don't know if that's easier. I overheard the conversation around two yesterday afternoon. I freaked and rushed around the city in a panic for a couple of hours. I actually started toward Maine before thinking of coming here. I checked into a fleabag hotel in Virginia around two in the morning, but to be honest I didn't sleep very well."

He stood, needing to put some distance between them. "I'll heat some soup. Give me your keys and I'll put your car in the shed so it'll be out of sight. I don't think anyone will look for you here, but better safe than sorry."

She grabbed his arm, and unwanted warmth shot through his body.

"Thanks, Jericho." Her voice was small but earnest. "You're saving my life."

Uncomfortable with her thanks and even more uncomfortable with the way his body responded to the feel of her hand on his forearm, he snapped, determined to set her straight so she didn't get the wrong idea about his motives. "I'm not doing it for you. I'm repaying a debt."

"What debt?"

"Your parents helped Jeanette after her parents died and she had nowhere to go. So I'm helping you. When this is over we'll be even and I'll never have to lay eyes on you again."

Telling himself it couldn't possibly be pain he saw on her face, he stalked to the kitchen to warm up some soup. The sooner he got her fed and safely in the guest room, the better off he'd be. But somehow he had the feeling getting her out of his mind wasn't going to be as easy as getting her out of his sight tonight.

Chapter Two

Camille looked around the kitchen as she sipped the chicken and rice soup. Spacious and up-to-date, the room still managed to remain in keeping with the rest of the farmhouse. The pink-and-green-flowered curtains and matching canisters on the soapstone countertops reminded her that Jericho may live alone now but there had been a woman here. Jeanette.

Camille closed her eyes on a wave of guilt. Had she really turned her back on her best friend simply because she'd fallen in love? True, Jeanette had broken Rodney's heart, but she hadn't meant to. She'd let him down as easily as she could. Yet Camille had refused to forgive her friend. She'd rejected every one of Jeanette's overtures. Now Jeanette was gone and Camille would never be able to make things right between them.

Sorrow and regret filled her, turning her stomach.

She put down her spoon, her appetite gone. The irony of her present situation didn't escape her. She'd forced Jeanette out of her life because she'd chosen Jericho over Rodney, and now Camille was forcing herself into Jericho's life. He was letting her stay only because of Jeanette.

"Is something wrong with the soup?" Jericho asked, his voice hard. It was as if he was waiting for her to complain. Was he looking for an excuse to throw her out? There was no way she would give him one.

She squelched a sigh, swallowed more soup, then looked at her reluctant host. "No. It's delicious. It tastes too good to have come from a can."

The corners of his mouth turned down. "A friend of mine is a chef."

Male or female? For some insane reason the thought of another woman bustling around this kitchen disturbed her. She shoved that feeling, whatever it was, aside. She was a guest here. Her welcome was tenuous at best. She didn't have the right to start asking questions about Jericho's life. Still a part of her was curious about the man her friend had fallen so hard for. What was it about him that had been so appealing that it had caused Jeanette to break off her engagement to Camille's brother?

One thing Camille now knew: Jericho was dependable. He might not like her—heck, he hated her—but he'd been willing to provide her with a safe haven. More than that, he hadn't asked for a thing in return. True, he viewed it as repaying a debt, but if there was a debt, it wasn't his to pay.

Her spoon clanked against the bowl, and she realized she'd been so lost in her thoughts she hadn't been aware she'd been eating.

"More?" Jericho asked.

She shook her head, then caught herself. Hadn't her mother drilled into her the proper way to respond to a question? She must be even more tired than she thought. The soft light and the warmth of the room had lulled her into a calm she hadn't felt since she'd first discovered the criminal activity at her firm. "No, thank you."

She wiped her mouth with her napkin and pushed away from the table. Grabbing her bowl, she stood, intending to wash her dishes in the ceramic farm sink beneath the large window. Even from across the room she could see the sink was empty; she didn't want to leave a mess for Jericho to clean up later. Nor did she want to leave him with the impression that she was the spoiled rich girl he thought she was.

"I'll take care of this," he said, taking her bowl from her.

"That's not necessary."

"I insist." His tone ended all discussion.

"Thanks." She waited quietly as he washed her dishes, wiped them dry and placed them in the cabinet beside the sink.

He leaned against the counter and stared at her. For all his concern about feeding her, his eyes were remarkably cold, his voice remote. "I'll show you where you can bunk while you're here."

Bunk. A cowboy word. Not a word she was used to hearing on Wall Street. It had a nice ring to it. Soothing. It conjured up images of honorable men on the range who would ensure no harm came to anyone. Hopefully, this horse ranch in North Carolina and its owner could provide the protection she needed until the danger passed. And it had to pass, didn't it? She forced that worry away. She was safe for now, and that was what she would focus on.

Camille followed Jericho through a narrow hall and up a flight of stairs. A gray and burgundy runner centered on the old oak risers muffled their footsteps. The house wasn't as large as the Chicago Gold Coast mansion where she'd grown up, but it was a good size and quite cozy. Jericho led her past a closed door and paused briefly before a second.

He opened the door a few inches. "This is the guest bathroom."

She caught a glimpse of a white pedestal sink before he closed the door.

He opened a door farther down the hall, and she hurried to catch up with him. "Linen closet." He pulled out towels, folded sheets and two blankets, then handed them to her before shutting the door with a definite click. What? Did he think she would steal his linen?

He crossed the hall and opened another door but didn't step inside. "You'll be sleeping here. This is the only bed you're welcome in."

She gasped, and her cheeks heated with remembered embarrassment. Before she could think up a suitable reply, he'd vanished back down the hall. She heard the stairs creak under his feet, and a minute later a door slammed.

Truthfully there was nothing she could say to justify her behavior all those years ago. She had bribed her way into his hotel room and gotten into his bed. Not one of her proudest moments. She hadn't actually planned to seduce him. She just wanted to prove to Jeanette that

Jericho wasn't the man he claimed to be so Jeanette would return to Rodney and things would get back to the way they were supposed to be. She'd expected Jericho to take her up on her offer. Then she would be able to tell Jeanette what he'd been willing to do.

She'd been wrong. Jericho had taken one look at her, his face twisted with disgust, and left the room. She'd waited for Jeanette to confront her about her behavior, but she never had. Apparently Jericho had never told Jeanette about the incident. That one horrible secret had weighed Camille down for years and was one of the reasons she'd worried Jericho would turn her away.

Physically and mentally exhausted, and sick and tired of the thoughts that continuously circled her mind, Camille removed her shoes and dropped onto the bare mattress. It was firm and cool and seemed to wrap her with comfort. She'd put on the sheets in a minute. She just needed to close her eyes for a bit and block out everything.

After a while, she forced herself to get up before she fell into a deep sleep. She grabbed her towels and crept to the bathroom. When she found a new toothbrush and toothpaste inside the mirrored medicine cabinet, she nearly shouted for joy. It seemed an eternity since she'd performed her simple grooming routine.

She had a brief internal debate, then concluded that she could not possibly wear her underwear a third straight day. Two days in a row was bad enough. Slipping off her panties and bra, she washed them by hand and left them on the side of the tub to dry. She'd slept in her clothes last night, and it looked like she would be doing the same again since she didn't think Jericho would lend her a T-shirt to sleep in. She was lucky he was letting her stay in his house. She wouldn't push it by asking for some of his clothes. The idea of wearing something that belonged to him seemed too intimate anyway, so she couldn't summon the nerve to ask him. Still, she was relieved to know she didn't have to be ready to flee at a moment's notice. She was safe. That had to count for something.

Jericho closed the shed door, then walked across the yard to the barn, Shadow circling his heels. The dog had been a surprise birthday present from Jeanette. Her last gift to him. The pesky dog provided the only type of companionship Jericho wanted even if Shadow couldn't follow the simplest command.

Shadow didn't make subtle hints about getting on with his life or give unsolicited advice. The dog didn't presume to know what Jeanette would have wanted for him. The dog simply let Jericho be himself, feeling—or as the case may be, not feeling—whatever he wanted.

Jericho went to each stall, checking on the horses. Although he'd settled them for the night before Camille's sudden appearance, he needed distance from the woman who'd invaded his home, disrupting the solitary life he now preferred.

There was a time when he'd been a people person. He'd enjoyed the company of others and had entertained for both business and pleasure. His house had been the gathering place for his friends and he'd held many an impromptu party. His parents had raised him to seize the day. He'd embraced his father's mantra: *No day is more important than this one. No breath more valuable than the one you are taking. Make each moment count.*

He'd done that. He'd wrung every bit of pleasure out

of his life. He'd met Jeanette while he'd been visiting his sister in Chicago. One look was all it had taken for him to realize they were made for each other. She'd made him appreciate his life even more. He'd been content before he'd met her, but once they'd married, his joy had known no bounds.

When she died from complications from her pregnancy, she'd taken the best part of him with her. He no longer felt joy with each day and struggled to find value in each breath. He'd be the first to admit that he'd become a hermit. He'd shrunk his business, dismissing all but two ranch hands and limiting his interactions with them to the barest minimum. He'd removed himself from the world, and only the most stubborn of his friends insisted on coming to the ranch. He had managed to survive their occasional intrusions. Somehow he knew he wasn't going to deal with Camille's constant presence in the same way.

Turning out the lights, he made his way back to the house. The moon was bright, lighting his way. Not that he needed it. He'd grown up on this piece of land and knew it like the back of his hand. When times had gotten tough, his grandparents had sold off all but the fifteen acres surrounding the house. Over the years, his parents bought back thirty acres. Jericho had worked hard to earn money and had bought back the remaining 340 acres that had been part of the Joneses' original property. He'd intended to purchase two hundred additional acres last year, but the desire to expand and build upon what had once belonged to his forefathers had died on a clear February morning along with all of his other dreams.

The kitchen was dark, but he didn't switch on the

light. He could still picture Camille sitting at the table sipping her soup despite himself. As a proud woman, she wouldn't appreciate knowing just how frayed she'd looked. The flight from danger and all the worry had stripped away her haughtiness, leaving her almost humble. No doubt after a good night's sleep her usual self-centered personality would rear its ugly head.

Not that Camille was ugly. Far from it. With light brown skin, high cheekbones, full lips and hazel eyes, she had a face that was far too beautiful to be considered anything short of remarkable. Of course, she personified the saying about beauty being skin deep. He knew the ugliness that lurked beneath the surface better than anyone. Despite how vulnerable she'd appeared tonight, he wouldn't fool himself into thinking she'd changed.

He had no intention of turning his life upside down just because she'd dropped in out of nowhere, disturbing his solitude. He was not about to alter one single thing in his life just to suit her. If she thought for a moment that he was going to entertain her, she had another thought coming. In fact, the less he saw of her, the better off he would be.

That settled, he climbed the stairs and went to his lonely bed wondering if tonight would be the night he would finally be able to sleep.

Camille stretched and yawned, then burrowed deeper into her pillow, pleased that her neighbors had decided to keep down the noise. She smiled and tried to resume her dream before reality hit. She wasn't in New York; she was on the run for her life. Her eyes flew open and she bolted upright, looking around the room. Memories of last night flooded her mind and her heart settled, gradually slowing to a normal beat.

She was safe. Jericho had welcomed her into his home. *Welcome* might be overstating things, but he had said she could stay, something that had been in doubt for a few harrowing minutes there. What would she do if he changed his mind? She'd taken him by surprise last night and he hadn't had time to consider his answer. Perhaps having slept on it, he'd decide he didn't really want her around.

And now that she thought about it, he hadn't said she could stay until she was safe. He had agreed only to let her spend the night. Perhaps he would press her to leave today. Then what would she do?

She wouldn't let that happen. She'd just make sure he didn't change his mind. The ranch was big and no doubt kept him busy. He probably didn't have time to do everything. Maybe there was something she could do around the house to help him and thereby earn her keep. Some way she could be of value to him.

She flashed back to the first time they'd met at a reception hosted by her father's law firm to celebrate his being appointed to the federal appellate court. Jericho had tagged along with his sister, who was working at the firm the summer after her second year in law school. He'd been charming and outgoing. Friendly. Then Jeanette had walked into the room. Camille had introduced them and the rest, as the saying went, had been history.

Only the history between her and Jericho had turned bitter. If she didn't change the way they interacted, she could be out on her ear and searching for another sanctuary. There wasn't one. If there had been, she would have gone there instead.

She put the pillow against the headboard and then leaned back. It would be easier if she didn't dislike him so much. He'd swept in and ruined her brother's engagement without a second thought, then whisked Jeanette halfway across the country. Camille had been the one her heartbroken brother had turned to. She'd never forget the pain she'd felt at seeing her brother in tears. All because of Jericho Jones.

Still, she was at his mercy so she needed to keep her contempt to herself. Surely she could do that. She was discovering previously unknown acting skills. She'd managed to keep her knowledge about Donald Wilcox's criminal activity from him. She'd been cordial and professional, even enduring business dinners with him. Certainly she could maintain a similar facade with Jericho.

She got up and made up her bed, then opened her door. A quick glance down the hall revealed that the other doors were closed. Was Jericho awake? She crossed the room and checked her watch. Given that it was 7:30 a.m., she imagined he was.

Padding across the wooden floor, she went to the tiny bathroom. She brushed her teeth, then got in the tub, letting the hot water ease the stress from her body. Even though she would have to wear her crumpled skirt and blouse for a third consecutive day, it wouldn't feel so bad if she was clean. The red silk had been a favorite of hers. She'd splurged on the designer suit and matching pumps two months ago. Now she'd be quite happy to never wear it again. In fact, when this was all over, she would donate it to a women's shelter.

She dried off and then slipped into her slightly damp underwear. Pulling on her skirt and blouse, she stepped into her shoes. It was too hot for the jacket, and she absolutely refused to wear pantyhose on a ranch or farm or whatever this was.

Her stomach growled. She took a quick look around the bathroom to be sure she hadn't left anything out of place. The room was small, but she had to admit she preferred the old-fashioned claw-foot tub to the Jacuzzi in her own spa-like bathroom.

She didn't call out to Jericho, knowing instinctively that he wasn't in the house. It felt too empty. Although she remembered where the kitchen was, she took a detour. Last night she'd been too nervous and then too relieved to notice much of anything. Now her curiosity got the better of her and she decided to look around.

She entered the living room and slid her finger across an end table, leaving a clean mark in the thin layer of dust. She picked up a framed photo, and her breath caught. It was a picture of Jericho and Jeanette. He was holding Jeanette in his lap as they sat in a tree swing. They were smiling and their eyes were lit with laughter. Suddenly feeling like a voyeur, Camille replaced the picture and hurried from the room into the kitchen. She'd ended her friendship with Jeanette, forfeiting the right to know about her life and her marriage.

If she was going to ensure Jericho allowed her to stay, she needed to prove her value to him. There probably wasn't any use for her skills as a financial wizard, but she could cook and clean for him.

Camille opened the refrigerator and groaned. The pickings were definitely slim. There were half a dozen eggs, a hunk of cheese, a carton of milk and half a bottle of orange juice. She didn't see how a man the size of Jericho managed on so little food. She rummaged through his pantry and found one onion. A two-egg omelet would be a start, but there was no way he would get full simply eating eggs.

"In for a penny, in for a pound," she muttered under her breath. She opened cabinets and canisters to see what she had to work with, finding flour, baking powder and sugar. Homemade pancakes along with the omelet would be a somewhat more substantial breakfast.

Humming to herself, she mixed the ingredients in a large bowl. Though she had always loved cooking, she hadn't made anything more involved than toast or a microwave meal in years. Being a rising star in the banking world required sacrifice and all of her time. Fortunately, cooking was like riding a bike, but without the sore calves. There was something soothing about pouring the batter onto a sizzling pan and watching golden pancakes materialize.

When they were done, she put the plate containing a dozen midsize pancakes in the oven to keep warm, then headed out the door. Jericho had to be somewhere. Hopefully, he would recognize her peace offering for what it was without her having to tell him.

She walked down the back stairs, surprised to see a brick patio surrounding an in-ground pool and hot tub. She skirted a table and chairs and hurried in the direction of a large building. Shadow was chasing a squirrel across the grass, having great fun. She doubted the squirrel found the game as amusing as he did. When the dog spotted her, he abandoned the squirrel and ran over, wagging his tail a mile a minute.

"Where's your master?" she asked. The dog cocked

his head, barked twice and sat on his haunches. He lifted his paw as if offering to shake. Clearly there was a failure to communicate.

She patted his head briefly. Shadow considered her for a moment, then raced around the yard as if searching for the squirrel so they could continue playing. Although she found the dog's antics amusing and could have watched him for hours, she was on a mission.

As Camille stepped into the stable, she inhaled the sweet smell of hay mingled with leather and pine. She expected to see horses, but the stalls were empty. Perhaps they were in a pasture or corral or whatever it was called. She needed to learn how to speak country.

She walked down the center aisle that separated the stalls until she reached the back of the building. Jericho was in a small room rubbing soap on a saddle. From the intense way he was scrubbing, she wouldn't be surprised if he rubbed a hole into the leather. The muscles on his arms bunched and flexed beneath his shirt.

She must have made a sound because he turned and looked up, one eyebrow raised. He stared at her without speaking, and she suddenly felt self-conscious. Instead of flinching the way she wanted, she raised her chin and spoke with a confidence she didn't feel. "I didn't mean to disturb you. I just wanted you to know I made breakfast."

He grunted, nodded toward a ceramic mug and turned back to his work. "I had coffee."

"Pancakes. And omelets." She twisted the hem of her blouse, unsure if she'd made the right decision. Naturally she started to babble, a habit she thought she'd overcome in finishing school. "Well, the pancakes are in the oven staying warm. I haven't made the eggs yet.

But I did grate the cheese and dice the onions. It'll only take a minute to throw them together."

He was silent for so long she didn't think he was going to answer. Finally he looked at her again, his eyes unreadable. "You don't have to cook for me."

"I don't mind," she rushed to assure him. "I like to cook."

He frowned, and her heart sank. Obviously she'd said the wrong thing. "I should have said I don't need you cooking for me."

She swallowed her hurt. She didn't like him, so why did it bother her that he didn't like her either? She'd never been the sensitive type. Apparently the stress of the situation was getting to her. "Okay. But since I already have, maybe you can eat this time? I would hate for good food to go to waste."

He stared at her so long it took monumental effort not to squirm. "Fine. This time."

She felt his eyes on her as he followed her to the house. Part of her wished she could throw away the food, but she'd been raised to know that wasting anything was sinful.

She cooked the omelets, pleased that she hadn't lost her ability to make them perfectly. After he washed his hands, he removed the platter of pancakes from the oven. He placed half on her plate and the other half on his own. She added the omelets, poured juice and joined him at the table.

"There's only butter. I couldn't find syrup."

"Don't have any." He cut his pancakes with the side of his fork. "I guess you'll have to make do, something new for a spoiled rich kid like you."

She swallowed the snarky reply on her lips. She

wasn't going to fight with him so he would have an excuse to put her out. Besides, she'd been insulted before. She'd endured slights both subtle and blatant. Women didn't make it to the top of her male-dominated field if they were shrinking violets. Most men resented her brains and her success. She'd shot down those she could and ignored those she couldn't.

She tucked into her breakfast, pleased to see that he was eating his without further comment. Now that she had a closer look at him, she realized he'd lost weight. He was still muscular and no doubt strong, but he could stand to put on a few pounds. Perhaps grief had stolen his appetite. Or maybe he didn't like to cook.

He'd told her he didn't need her to cook for him, but maybe he'd said that only because he was annoyed that she'd disturbed him. He certainly seemed to be enjoying his breakfast. Or maybe later on he planned to accuse her of being a pampered princess. Whatever, she wasn't going to give him an excuse to kick her out. She'd pull her weight while she was here.

They finished the meal in silence. When he'd eaten the last bit of eggs, he carried his dishes to the sink, gave her one last glance and left without saying a word.

She heaved a heavy sigh. At least he hadn't told her to leave.

Chapter Three

Camille washed the dishes, wiped the counters and table, and sat down. *Now what?*

She'd cleaned the kitchen from top to bottom, trying to distract herself from her situation, but it hadn't worked. No matter how busy her hands were, she couldn't keep her mind from circling back to her problem. People wanted her dead. Would they change their minds if they couldn't find her, or would they keep searching? Did the authorities have enough information to arrest Donald Wilcox and his hit men? And how would she find out?

She and Agent Delgado had been communicating by email. In the last one he'd sent, he'd told her not to write to him until he reached out to her. Although he didn't believe she was in danger, he'd wanted her to lie low. And then he'd been in that car accident. So now what should she do? What could she do? Nothing. She couldn't lie any lower than she was now.

But she couldn't just twiddle her thumbs. After a lifetime of being busy, Camille found the quiet and endless hours looming ahead of her a little disconcerting. If she didn't do something physical she would go out of her mind with worry. She would clean Jericho's house for him. But how would she manage to do it without studying the pictures or the various knickknacks and dredging up memories?

She searched through the kitchen cabinets until she found all the cleaning supplies she needed. Unwilling to stain her skirt, especially since it was all she had to wear, she tied a towel around her waist and set to work. She started in the front room, waxing the tables, careful to place every picture and lamp where it belonged. Her heart pinched with regret as she wiped the dust off pictures of Jeanette.

Camille had planned to forgive Jeanette and reconcile with her at some vague date in the future. Lately she'd begun to wonder whether there had been anything to forgive. Jeanette hadn't done anything wrong to Camille. If anything, Camille had been the one in need of forgiveness. But it was too late. Jeanette was gone so Camille couldn't make things right.

Regrets churning in her stomach, Camille finished cleaning the front room, then moved on to the dining room. Moving with precision, she dusted and wiped every nook and cranny, scrubbing until the room shone. Then she moved to the last room on the first floor, a study. She dusted the bookshelves and then proceeded to the writing desk.

"What are you doing in my office?"

Camille spun around, grabbing the top of a leather chair. She'd never been a particularly nervous person, but the stress of the last couple of days had rattled her until she was jumping at every little thing. She could understand being so hyperalert when she was in danger. But she was safe now.

At least she thought she was. Looking at Jericho made her wonder. Standing inside the door, his muscular arms folded across his equally muscular chest, his eyes narrowed, anger radiated off him in waves that shot across the room and crashed into her. Even though he was so furious he was vibrating, she still couldn't help but notice how incredibly handsome he was. How masculine. She told herself that her heart lurched in her chest because he'd startled her, but that was only partly true.

He raised an eyebrow, and she realized she hadn't answered his question so she replied, "Cleaning."

"Why?"

"I thought I could help you."

"What gave you the idea I needed or wanted your help?"

Her stomach sank. So much for being thoughtful. While she believed she was showing him how she could make his life better, hoping he'd be less inclined to change his mind about letting her stay here, her actions may have had the opposite effect. He still hadn't committed to a specific time frame for her stay, which would have given her a little peace of mind. Instead she was left in limbo, wondering if the next words out of his mouth would be the ones she dreaded hearing: *get out*. Of course now wasn't the time to try to get him to commit. Not when she was one false move from being tossed out on her ear.

"I...uh." Her voice faded out as nothing came to mind. At least nothing that wouldn't sound like criticism of his housekeeping skills.

"I'm sorry if the accommodations at the Double J don't meet the lofty standards you're accustomed to," he said, his lips barely moving. He didn't raise his voice. Somehow that made his fury even more pronounced. "But you barged in on my life and home, not the other way around."

"I'm sorry. I was just trying to show my appreciation."

"If you want to show your gratitude, then stay out of my way and out of my office. The less I see of you the better."

She nodded, too stunned to reply, then walked out of his office, careful not to brush against him.

Cursing under his breath, but loud enough for her to hear, he stormed through the hallway. Seconds later she heard the back door slam. Her shoulders slumped, and she sighed. Even though Jericho was gone, her stomach still churned like the Atlantic Ocean during a storm. She closed her eyes, trying to hold back hot tears. Crying never helped.

She heard whining, then felt a wet nose pushing against her hand. Shadow. She knelt and buried her face in the dog's fur. "I really messed up this time."

Shadow barked in reply, then swiped his tongue against her cheek. She hugged him once more, then pushed to her feet. She rinsed the mop, emptied the bucket and put the rest of the supplies where she found them. She needed to make herself scarce. Her three-inch heels weren't ideal for walking on a ranch, but she couldn't remain in the house.

* * *

Jericho saddled Diablo and rode across the field, the horse's hooves thundering against the ground. The spirited stallion loved racing, and Jericho gave him the freedom to do so. They shot across the acreage as if the hounds of hell were after them.

No matter how fast they went, Jericho couldn't outrun the sorrowful look on Camille's face when he'd lit into her. He knew she was scared and was probably trying to stay busy in order to keep from worrying about the people who wanted to kill her. She was literally running for her life and had come to him. Knowing that he disliked her, that couldn't have been easy. In fact, that was further proof of just how desperate and frightened she was.

It didn't matter that he didn't want her here. He'd told her she could stay. Implied in that statement was the promise that he would make her feel at least marginally welcome.

She was nervous and walking on eggshells and not only because she was in fear for her life. She was uneasy because of him. That idea turned his stomach. He'd never thought he'd see confident Camille as timid as she'd been that morning at breakfast. And he never wanted to see her that way again. He preferred the proud woman. That pride wouldn't allow her to take from him without giving something in return. He understood that. He was the same way. When he went back to the house, he'd apologize to her.

They might not like each other, but they were going to have to find a way to peacefully coexist. Keeping their interactions to a minimum would be key. And they needed to discuss how long she planned to stay here.

Not that he expected her to know for sure. But she had to have some idea when this would be over. They'd both feel better if they could establish how long they were going to be stuck with each other. And they needed to set up some ground rules.

Though he could have used a calmer tone, he was being honest when he said they needed to stay away from each other. Camille's very presence disturbed him. For the past year and a half he'd sleepwalked through his days. He'd been fine with that. Camille was changing that—changing him—simply by being around.

Her long legs were driving him crazy. He didn't like noticing her slender curves or the way her breasts rose when she took a deep breath. Watching her nibble on her bottom lip had the potential to send him sailing over the edge of reason.

He'd always known his sexual desire would return one day. He just hadn't expected Camille Parker to be the one to awaken it. The ferocity also startled him. He wasn't worried that his emotions would return or that his heart would open to Camille. He'd buried his heart with Jeanette. But still, there was no need to risk it. He couldn't survive another heartbreak.

After brushing Diablo, leading him to his stall and making sure he had fresh water, Jericho returned to the house. He wasn't looking forward to this conversation, but he was man enough to admit when he'd done wrong. Camille wasn't in the kitchen or the living room. But hadn't he practically banned her from the common areas of the house? Regret gnawed at his insides as he climbed the stairs to the second floor.

The door to the guest room was closed. He knocked softly. No response. He knocked again, this time more loudly. Still she didn't answer. Now he was the one shut out. Talk about poetic justice. After an internal debate about the propriety of opening her door without her permission, he turned the knob.

"Camille?" He called quietly in case she was asleep. He opened the door an inch and peeked inside. Her perfectly made-up bed was empty. He stepped inside and looked around. There was no sign of her. Surely she wouldn't have left. She didn't have anywhere else to go. It wasn't safe for her to use her credit cards. He'd been too angry to ask if she had cash. He had to find her and bring her back before she put herself in danger. The irony wasn't lost on him.

Cursing himself for being a thoughtless jerk, he raced down the stairs and out the back, crossed the grassy field, then yanked open the door of his shed. Her car remained where he'd parked it. A relieved breath whooshed from his chest. At least she had the good sense not to run away.

He closed and locked the door, then went through the house and to the front porch. Sitting down in one of the two wooden rockers that had been on the far corner of the porch for as long as he could remember, he set the chair in motion. He'd grown up hearing how his grandfather had carved them for his grandmother after she'd caught him talking with her main rival at the high school Christmas dance. After that, she'd ignored him for months. He'd shown up on her birthday with the two rockers and a marriage proposal. The apology gift had worked, and they'd married the week after graduation. Jericho rubbed his hand over the smooth wood that had stood the test of time and three generations of endless rocking and wondered if there was any more magic in the chairs.

The day was bright and sunny, and from his position he could see clear across his property to the road nearly a mile away. He couldn't recall the last time he'd simply sat here and let the warmth of the day wash over him and take his cares away. He didn't feel quite at peace, but that was fine. Peace was no longer something he sought or even deserved. Getting through the day without breaking down was enough for him.

Twenty minutes later he heard barking followed by feminine laughter. He scanned the area and watched as Camille and Shadow came into view. She threw a stick and Shadow chased it. A few seconds later the dog ran back to Camille. She reached for the branch, and the dog backed away. Then, treasure clasped firmly in his jaws, the dog ran a short distance away. He dropped the stick, raced back to Camille and sat on his haunches.

Camille laughed and rubbed the dog. "You're still missing the point. You're supposed to give the stick to me so I can throw it again."

Shadow barked, then ran in circles around the yard. Fetch was beyond his mental abilities. Camille went over to the stick and bent to pick it up again. Her skirt tightened over her round bottom, and Jericho's breath caught in his throat.

She turned and saw him. Even from a distance he noticed the way she stiffened and let the stick slip from her fingers. She continued toward the house slowly. The bubble of joy that had surrounded her mere seconds earlier popped. No doubt about it, she was uncomfortable around him.

He descended the front steps and walked in her direction. Shadow spotted him and raced over, his tail wagging. The dog circled Jericho, and then the traitor raced back to Camille.

She was barefoot and her shoes were dangling from her fingers. The heat must have gotten to her because she'd untucked her blouse and knotted the ends around her waist, revealing the smooth skin of her stomach. His mouth went dry at the sight, and he quickly looked away. He didn't understand how he could be aroused by a woman he didn't even like.

"I went for a walk. You didn't say I couldn't." Her chin jutted out defiantly, but the wariness in her eyes belied her confidence.

He'd never heard her sound so uncertain, and guilt smacked him like a fist to his jaw. "Did you enjoy yourself?"

Her eyes widened in apparent surprise, making him feel like an even bigger jerk. He didn't want her to be shocked that he could be courteous.

"Actually, yes. My walk gave me the opportunity to clear my head and think about things. I realize that I owe you an apology. I'm so sorry for barging into your home and overstepping my bounds. I see now how upsetting that can be."

He raised his hand to stop her. "No. If anyone should apologize it's me. I was wrong to tear into you like that. You were being thoughtful and I was an ungrateful jerk. Please forgive me."

She nodded but continued to stare at him. Clearly there was more she wanted to say, but she was unsure whether to take the risk. Having another person around was going to be a lot harder than he thought. "You have something to say?"

"About dinner." She nibbled on her lip. "I know you don't want me cooking for you, but you have to eat. I already took something out of the freezer to cook. Before… If you would prefer, we can eat separately."

"That's not necessary."

"But we need to eat."

"I meant the part about eating separately. We can eat dinner together like we did breakfast." It had been a stilted, awkward affair he'd hoped never to repeat, but she was in fear for her life. If sharing meals was what it took for her to become more at ease, then that's what he would do.

No matter how much he hated it.

Chapter Four

"Pass the peas," Camille said, even though she didn't want another spoonful. Truthfully she wasn't that fond of peas, but it was either peas or Brussels sprouts, which she detested. And she just couldn't take another moment of cold silence. For the past fifteen minutes she and Jericho had simply eaten dinner, speaking—or in his case, muttering—to each other only when necessary. Her nerves were frazzled enough as it was; now she was at the breaking point.

It wasn't as if she was unused to eating in relative quiet. She was a single woman who lived alone. But there was something decidedly uncomfortable about sitting across the table from someone, looking at the person when the two of you glanced up at the same time, and not speaking. Add that to the constant fear crawling up her spine, and, well, she was one second away from becoming a raving lunatic.

Shadow whined under the table, and Camille started to sneak him a piece of her fried chicken. Jericho's glare had her putting the bit of drumstick into her mouth instead.

There was a noise outside the window and she jumped.

"It's just raccoons." His voice was flat, lacking emotion.

"Oh." What in the world were they doing? The frown on Jericho's face had her swallowing that question along with the nasty peas. If she had her way, she'd be anywhere but here, but since that wasn't an option, she had to make the best of it. She'd fill the silence the best way she knew how.

In her experience, people enjoyed talking about themselves and their successes. There was no reason to believe Jericho would be any different. "This is a nice ranch. How big is it?"

He didn't look up. "Three hundred and eighty-five acres."

She swallowed her sigh. It was almost as difficult as downing the peas. He wasn't being outwardly hostile, but still. She was making an effort, which was more than she could say for him. She decided to try again.

"I love the pool area. It's so beautiful. So unexpected." There. That was nice and complimentary. And it wasn't exactly a lie. If he would tend the landscaping it would be showstopping.

"Thanks."

That was it? He couldn't think of one other thing to say that might help carry the conversation.

She took another bite of chicken, chewing slowly as her mind searched for topics to fill the silence. There

was only so much she could say about pools. Maybe
she should bring up the charming aspects of country life. Surely that would get him to give more than
one-word answers. "I just thought you'd have a swimming hole."

"Swimming hole?" He echoed, sounding confused.
She wondered if he had even been listening to her.

"It's something I read about in a book. It always
sounded so nice." She forced a smile. She loved romances and read them every chance she got, which
wasn't often. Judging by the way her love life was going,
the closest she was going to get to a happily-ever-after
was between the covers of a book. Of course, since she
was running for her life and might not get an ever-after
of any kind, finding Mr. Right was pretty low on her
priority list. In fact, the only item on her list was staying alive. "Do you have a swimming hole on the ranch?"

"Yes." He was back to one-word answers.

Forget this. Clearly Jericho wasn't interested in having a conversation. It wasn't worth the effort to try to
be friendly to someone who wasn't inclined to do the
same. Her appetite gone, she tossed her napkin onto her
plate, then although it was incredibly rude and not at all
in keeping with her upbringing, stood. "I don't think
I can eat another bite. I'm going to wash these dishes
and head up to bed. Good night."

When she was finished cleaning up, she felt Jericho's eyes on her as she left the room, but she didn't
turn around. What would be the point? They were enemies. She'd just hoped that his earlier friendliness, such
as it was, meant that he'd at least make an effort to be
cordial. Not that she expected them to become friends.
She still hated him. She'd thought they could manage

a bit of civility. She'd been wrong. Apparently she was the only one willing to fake it. She wouldn't make that mistake again.

Jericho watched as Camille walked out. Why hadn't he been able to give her a break? He'd seen just how jittery she was, jumping at every sound. Her eyes had darted around the room furtively, as if some assassin was lurking in the shadows. No doubt she was checking under her bed and searching through the closet for killers right now.

The skittish woman was so different from the person he'd met all those years ago in Chicago. That Camille had been confident to the point of being arrogant. He flashed back to the reception at her father's law firm. He and Camille had met by the buffet table. It hadn't taken longer than ten minutes for him to tell she was driven to succeed to the exclusion of everything else. She didn't have any hobbies to speak of and her conversation revolved around her job and salary. He believed in hard work, but he knew life needed to be balanced. There had to be time for hanging out with friends and having fun. She hadn't seen the need for pleasure in life.

He'd been about to excuse himself when Jeanette approached them. Even now his heart skipped a beat as he remembered just how beautiful she'd been in her floral dress. She'd smiled at him, and he'd sworn he could hear angels sing. Camille had introduced them, then spotted someone across the room she needed to speak to. He'd been so struck by Jeanette that he'd barely noticed Camille leave.

Memories of his life with Jeanette swirled around him. He cut them off. No matter how hard he tried limiting his thinking to the good times, the memory of her lying in a puddle of blood always came back. The agony of losing her and their baby haunted him day and night.

In a way he could relate to Camille. Part of him understood her need to distract herself from the reality that someone was hunting her down by engaging in annoying chatter. Heck, he drove himself to exhaustion every day in a futile attempt to keep his thoughts under control.

He heard her moving around in her room and glanced at the clock. Seven thirty. There was no way in the world she was sleepy at this hour. She just wanted to get away from him. He listened to her pace from windows to door for a few more minutes, then reluctantly rose.

Shadow lifted his head.

"Stay."

The dog hopped to his feet and raced around Jericho's legs. Although the dog would make a nice distraction while Jericho went to talk to Camille, he knew Shadow would prefer to run around outside. So Jericho let the dog out and resisted the urge to follow him into the summer evening.

He climbed the stairs and knocked softly on the partially open door. Camille had been peering out the window. She jumped and turned, one hand pressed against her chest. Her eyes were wide, and her mouth was open as if she was about to scream.

"It's just me." Her visible panic once again made him feel guilty for his earlier treatment of her. He needed to think of her as a woman in fear and not someone he detested. "You're safe here. You know that, right?"

She stood erect and lifted her chin in an attempt to appear strong. He could tell her that he'd seen her fear—

heck, she was shaking like a leaf—but he decided not to mention it.

"Sure."

She didn't sound convinced. He blew out a breath. "How about sitting outside for a bit?"

Either she didn't hear the reluctance in his voice or she was scared enough to ignore it. Either way, in less time than it took the words to leave his mouth, she'd flown across the room and they'd descended the stairs.

Now they were seated on the patio beside the pool. Shadow trotted over and placed his head on Camille's lap.

"Shadow, no," Jericho said. The dog barked once, then turned his attention back to Camille.

"I don't mind." She scratched Shadow's head, and the dog began wagging his tail so hard his lower body moved from side to side. "Who's a good boy?"

Shadow barked and then licked Camille's chin. Camille laughed, and something in Jericho's chest started to shake loose. Warmth flickered inside him, but he snuffed it out.

The fact that she liked dogs didn't change his opinion of her. Still, the woman letting the dog slobber all over her face didn't fit the image of the Camille Parker in his memory. That Camille was selfish and conniving and as cold as the ice encasing his heart.

"Thanks for sitting with me. My rational mind knows there is absolutely no way anyone can find me here, but..." She sighed and her voice faded away.

"But you can't believe it entirely, so you're still scared."

"Exactly."

She leaned back in her chair and closed her eyes. He

interpreted that to mean she didn't have anything else to say. The silence wasn't entirely awkward even if it was miles away from being comfortable. But he managed to keep his dislike buried far beneath the surface, at least for now.

She sprang up suddenly, her body as stiff as a board. "I hope my family isn't worried about me. I didn't get a chance to call them before I left."

"Do you talk to them often?"

"Yes and no. Rodney and I talk a few times a week. But one of his fraternity brothers is getting married in the Bahamas Saturday, so he's out of the country this week."

"Then he probably won't plan on talking to you."

"True."

"What about your parents?"

"I speak with them every Sunday, but nothing personal."

He stared at her. The sun hadn't quite set when they'd come outside, so he hadn't bothered to turn on the lights. Now her expression was hidden by shadows. "How can conversations with your parents not be personal?"

"It takes a certain level of skill that only comes with years of practice." Her voice was bitter, yet he heard pain there, as well. "We talk about work and setting professional goals. I can't remember a time when my parents weren't asking me where I saw myself in five years. Talking to them is a never-ending job interview."

She sighed. "All my parents care about is professional success and money. In a way I understand because they came from impoverished families. They know what it's like to not know where your next meal is coming from. But they never let Rodney and me just be kids. We couldn't do things just because they were fun. Everything we did had to be geared toward making money. I guess I started looking at everything that way, thinking that everyone always acted for their own personal gain."

Was there an apology in there?

He'd met the elder Parkers only a couple of times, and that had been years ago. He'd gotten the impression that they were driven to succeed at the expense of everything else, and it was a characteristic he'd attributed to Camille, as well. Until this very second he hadn't given a thought to how she'd been raised or the way it impacted her thinking.

The day he'd met Jeanette and Camille, he'd been struck by the close friendship they'd shared. They'd loved each other like sisters. Protected each other. If Camille had believed Jericho was trying to get Jeanette's money, she'd do everything she could to protect Jeanette, including coming between Jericho and Jeanette. Camille had been wrong about him, but given the way she'd been raised, perhaps he could give her a pass on that. Perhaps.

"You don't think the people who are after me would go after my parents or Rodney, do you?"

"No. There would be no point." At least he hoped they wouldn't harm her family. He didn't know anything about these people. But there was no sense in getting her all worked up since there wasn't a thing she could do. "Harming a sitting federal justice or his prominent surgeon wife seems like a big risk to take. It would bring lots of attention. And your brother is out of the country and out of reach."

"I hope you're right."

"I am." Jericho hoped. "And since your brother is hanging with his friends, he might not miss you right away. And it sounds like your parents won't worry if you miss one phone call."

She shrugged. "Maybe."

"How will you know when it's safe to return home?"

"I don't know. Agent Delgado and I had been keeping in touch by email. Now I'm not sure if I can trust him anymore. Even if he didn't sell me out, someone in his office did. And I'm not convinced his accident really was an accident."

"Then we'll have to play it by ear. Right now all you can do is wait here."

"Wait here," she repeated, sounding as though it was just this side of torture. Maybe to her it was. But then, having her around wasn't a day at the beach for him either.

Camille lay in bed, listening to the sounds of the house. Jericho was moving around in his room. He was pretty quiet, but she was a light sleeper. The thought of getting out of bed flitted through her mind, but she swatted it aside. She didn't want to disturb his morning routine. Besides, lying in bed and awakening gradually was a welcome change from her usual routine of jumping up at the crack of dawn, showering so quickly she barely got wet, then hopping into a suit and heels before racing out the door, travel mug in hand. Now that she was at Jericho's ranch, it wasn't as if she had anything pressing to do.

Truth be told, she wasn't looking forward to putting on her skirt and blouse yet again. She was so sick of wearing the same outfit, she was considering tossing it into the fireplace and putting it out of her misery. But she couldn't wrap herself in sheets. Jericho might think that she was out to seduce him again, and things between them would go south fast. She'd just have to pretend her suit was her old school uniform and that it was perfectly normal to wear the same skirt and blouse for days on end.

Her stomach twisted as she recalled her foolish attempt all those years ago to trick Jericho into revealing his true colors. She'd been so sure he was only after Jeanette's money. After all, who fell in love and got engaged after only a month?

Jericho and Jeanette—that's who. And as for showing his true character, he was doing that now. He was dependable. Noble. Acknowledging that didn't make them friends. But it did help her to admit she'd been wrong about him and his reasons for marrying Jeanette. And it did help her dial back her fear a little. Not enough to relax, but maybe enough to stop looking over her shoulder every seven seconds.

The sound of the back door closing was the impetus she needed to get up. Pulling on her despised skirt, she crossed the short hall. She opened the bathroom door and gasped. A pile of men's clothes was balanced on the edge of the bathtub. There were a couple of T-shirts and two pairs of basketball shorts. They weren't the height of fashion, but they would be a wonderful change of pace. Unexpected tears burned her eyes at Jericho's kindness. The cynical part of her reasoned that he'd lent her the clothes only because he couldn't stand to see her wearing her wrinkled suit one more day, but she refused to let that part diminish the joy his act awakened in her.

She sang softly as she bathed. The shower was the only place she'd sung since she was a freshman in high school and planned to audition for the student and faculty production of *The Wiz*. Unfortunately, her parents had discovered her plans and forbid her to do something so frivolous.

Throughout her childhood, none of her interests had made them proud. But they'd nearly popped their proverbial buttons when she landed a job in the financial sector. Not only was she making a ton of money, but her job actually dealt with money. To the Parkers, there was nothing greater. For the longest time she'd believed as they had, reaching for the brass—no, platinum—ring. She'd worked from sunup to late into the night. She'd spent her weekends working, no longer pursuing her interests. And where had that single-minded devotion gotten her? Hiding out on a ranch with a man who hated her while hired assassins sought to wipe her off the face of the earth.

She didn't know how it happened, but somewhere along the way she'd turned into her parents, defining success by how high she climbed at work and how much money she earned. When she'd been young, she'd enjoyed baking. She couldn't remember the last time she'd whipped up a batch of cookies just for the fun of it. Truth be told, she couldn't recall the last time she'd done anything just for fun. Well, no more. If she survived this, she was going to start living—no, loving—her life.

She took her time as she dressed, savoring the feel of the clean clothes against her skin. She inhaled deeply and imagined she could smell Jericho's male scent mingled in with the floral perfume of the laundry detergent. Wait—what could she possibly be thinking? Why in the world would she have such ridiculous notions about Jericho Jones of all people? They were combatants who'd decided to try being nice to each other. No more than that.

After she finished dressing, she darted down the stairs and out the door in search of Jericho.

His baritone voice, perfect for a rancher, came from the direction of the corral, and she followed it. Having grown up in Chicago and lived in New York, she was unused to seeing so much lush green grass or the small animals frolicking around the property. And she couldn't get over the smell. The air was so sweet and fresh, the day so perfect that nothing could possibly go wrong.

Camille gave a most unladylike snort at her fanciful thoughts. If she wasn't careful she'd be spouting poetry next.

When she reached the white fence, she put her foot on the bottom rail and leaned her arms against the top. Jericho was riding a beautiful brown horse in tight circles. She watched him for a moment, caught up in the very grace of the man.

He was dressed in jeans so faded they were white in places. They emphasized his well-defined thighs so well they could have been custom-made for him. With a faded plaid shirt taut across his broad chest, he was every woman's cowboy dream come to life. Not that she would ever admit to a hankering for cowboys.

Jericho looked up and saw her staring. He guided the horse over to the fence. "I see you found the clothes."

Telling her foolish heart to calm down, she nodded. "Yes. Thanks. I think I would have gone out of my mind if I had to wear that suit one more day."

"I should have thought of it sooner. Sorry I don't have anything that would fit you better. It was hard, but I gave away Jeanette's clothes."

"She had such a generous heart. That's what she would have wanted you to do."

He nodded and his eyes took on a faraway look. Was he thinking about Jeanette? She'd been so loving and kind, a better person than Camille could ever hope to be. And Camille had just thrown away her friendship, not recognizing its true value.

Camille stood straight and looked into Jericho's eyes. "I know I said it before, but I want you to know how much I appreciate your letting me stay here. If our situations were reversed, I'm not sure I'd be as gracious. In fact, I'm sure I wouldn't be. So thanks, Jericho."

He seemed surprised by her words and maybe a little uncomfortable. Obviously, he hadn't expected her to be so humble. He nodded and cleared his throat before looking at her high-heeled shoes. "We'll have to make a trip into town today and get you some clothes and shoes. Probably a few other things, as well."

"Do you think it's safe to leave here?" Camille spread her arms, encompassing the expanse of land. There was nothing but green grass and rolling hills as far as the eye could see. And not another soul around. But if they went into town someone would spot her. And it wasn't as if she would recognize the people looking for her. She hadn't seen their faces. She didn't know how many there were. And come to think of it, the killer could be a woman. And although she wouldn't recognize them, they knew exactly what she looked like. She'd be a sitting duck in town.

"You'll be perfectly safe. Remember, no one in New

York knows about me. And you don't have a connection to Sweet Briar so there's no reason for them to look here."

That was true. And hadn't she just promised herself to stop jumping at every shadow? Not to mention that there were certain items she couldn't do without. But she had a limited budget. She'd have to make wise choices and buy only what was necessary. A few T-shirts, underwear and a couple of pairs of shorts ought to be enough. "You're right. I'm ready when you are."

"I'll meet you by the truck in about ten."

Fifteen minutes later she was looking out the window of his pickup as they drove down the driveway. She'd been racing for her life when she'd arrived, and the last thing on her mind had been the scenery. Her short walk the other day had been nice, but she hadn't seen much of the Double J.

She saw several stands of trees spaced so randomly they couldn't have been put there by a landscaper.

A flock of birds flew through the air, swooping occasionally as if playing a game as they enjoyed this spectacular day.

Impossible.

"What's impossible?"

Heat crept up her cheeks, and she spun in her seat and looked at Jericho. "Did I say that out loud?"

He had one hand draped over the steering wheel. He glanced at her and nodded. "You did. But if you answer my question it won't look like you're talking to yourself."

She chuckled. "I was just thinking that the birds were enjoying themselves."

"I don't see why that would be impossible."

She hid her surprise. Part of her had expected him to mock her whimsy. He was surprising her at every turn. She was coming to believe she'd misjudged him before. Of course, that realization sat like a rock in her stomach. Perhaps she should stop expecting the worst from him.

They drove in silence for a while, but it was surprisingly comfortable and she didn't feel compelled to fill the quiet with mindless chatter. After about forty minutes they reached town. The main street was absolutely charming. Flower boxes overflowed with blooms in various colors and shapes. Mature trees swayed in the gentle breeze. The street was pristine, and the sidewalks looked as if they had been recently swept. Not even a gum wrapper lay on the ground. The place was postcard perfect. It was so different from New York that she blinked to make sure she wasn't imagining things.

The town was awakening and people began filling the streets, walking as if they didn't have a care in the world. Several men were gathered in front of a barbershop complete with the old-fashioned striped pole. One man looked up and then nudged the others. They all seemed to take an inordinate interest in Jericho. A woman walking into a candy store stopped and stared as they drove by. Jericho didn't appear to notice, but the attention made Camille's skin crawl. She blew out a breath and reminded herself that she was safe. Besides, Jericho appeared to be the one drawing their attention, not her.

"I bet you can't wait to get some clothes."

"Yes." Although she was grateful for what Jericho had provided, she'd feel more comfortable in women's clothes that fit better.

"There's a boutique on the corner that's popular with

tourists. You should be able to find something acceptable there."

At one time such a store might be a place she'd like to check out. Now? Not a chance. "I would prefer someplace a little less expensive."

The way he looked at her made her wonder if she'd sprouted a mole with a long hair on her nose. She'd arrived in a suit that cost thousands, so she could understand his shock. "I only have a few hundred dollars on me. I need to stretch my money as far as possible. I can't use my credit cards because they can be traced, so I'm going to go for quantity over quality."

"Gotcha. I seem to remember a little store that has reasonably priced women's clothes a couple of blocks from here."

"You remember?"

"There's no need for me to go there any longer."

Camille cringed. How could she be so stupid? "Right."

They drove another block and Jericho parked in front of a Victorian house that had been converted into a shop. The red brick building was well kept. There was a discreet sign in the window advertising Clothes by Hannah. Camille sighed with relief. She'd envisioned a run-down building and a sign with missing letters advertising a sale. If the clothes matched the classy exterior, she was guaranteed to find something stylish she could afford in her tight budget.

She opened the front door and a bell sounded.

"I'll be right with you. Feel free to look around," a female voice called from the back of the store.

Camille looked over at Jericho, who was standing just inside the door. "I'll be okay if you want to leave."

He shook his head and stepped beside her. His masculine scent wrapped around her, and she barely resisted the urge to lean in closer. One corner of his mouth lifted in a half smile, and her heart skipped a crazy beat. "I'm good here."

"Great," she croaked, and he raised one of his eyebrows. She hoped he couldn't tell how his nearness was beginning to affect her.

There were racks of dresses, skirts, blouses and shorts in various styles. The clothes were grouped by color as well, which made it easy for her to zero in on her favorite shades of orange, blue and green.

She grabbed an aqua shirt in her size and fingered the fabric. It was of good quality and the stitching was neat and strong. Camille looked at the price and felt the color rush from her face. Although the blouse wasn't expensive—indeed, given how well made the top was, it was a steal at twice the price—she couldn't afford it. Sighing, she replaced it on the rack.

"What's wrong? Don't you like it?"

"It's beautiful. But I can't afford it." She inhaled deeply. "Is there a discount store around?"

"We don't need to go to a discount store."

Hot tears burned her eyes. Did he think she didn't want these pretty clothes? "I told you. I have to make my money last. I need to find cheaper clothes."

"That's not necessary. I'm buying."

Chapter Five

"No, you're not." Camille folded her arms over her chest and lifted her chin. She was acting like a six-year-old but didn't care because she was starting to feel like one. She was dependent on Jericho for shelter, food and even protection if it came down to that. No way was she going to become indebted to him for clothing.

"Sorry to keep you waiting," the shop attendant said as she entered the front of the store. Immaculately dressed, the woman smiled warmly at them. She didn't even blink an eye at Camille's ill-fitting men's clothing. "I'm Hannah. How can I help you?"

"I'm sorry. You can't. Not today. Your clothes are lovely, but I have to go."

Camille tried to brush past Jericho, but he grabbed her elbow and held her just tight enough so that she couldn't leave without making a scene. Clearly he didn't know she was channeling her inner first-grader and was on the verge of having a tantrum. He smiled at the saleswoman. "Give us a second, would you?"

"Certainly." The woman walked away and began untangling bracelets hanging on a display rack on the other side of the room.

Camille pasted on a saccharine smile. But she didn't bother disguising the fury in her voice even if she did whisper. She knew better than to let outsiders witness a private dispute. Jericho wasn't family, but this matter was definitely private. "I don't need your charity."

"Of course you do." She thought he'd be offended by her tone, but his smile was firmly in place. Unlike hers, his appeared genuine. She couldn't imagine what was behind his change of heart. "You're staying in my home and eating my food, such as it is."

"Exactly. That's bad enough. I won't compound the problem by mooching clothes from you."

"Is that what you think you're doing? Mooching? Do you somehow think you're taking advantage of me?"

She nodded, and to her shame, tears pricked her eyes. *Please don't let them fall.* "I know you hate me and don't really want to help me. You're only doing it because of Jeanette. Because you think you owe my family."

He was silent for a long moment. When he spoke, his voice was gruff and yet somehow gentle. "Maybe I am, but you only came to me because of Jeanette, right?"

She nodded.

"As far as hating you…" He blew out a breath and shoved his hands in the pockets of his jeans. "It's not as easy now that I see you as an actual flesh-and-blood person as it was when you were the monster I remembered. You know?"

She understood. She was starting to see Jericho in an entirely different light, too, and wasn't any more comfortable about it than he was. She especially wasn't pleased about the physical attraction, but hopefully it was just due to the circumstances.

"So why don't you let me buy these clothes for you, okay?"

She sniffed. "I hate this."

"I know. But it's not as if you don't have money. You do. If it will make you feel better, you can pay me back."

"I will. Every cent plus interest."

"Damn straight." He smiled, making it easier for her pride to take him up on his offer.

"Is everything okay?" Hannah asked as she returned to them, looking back and forth between Camille and Jericho.

"Perfect. I love these clothes."

"Thanks. I designed a lot of them myself. What are you looking for?"

Camille exhaled. "Everything."

Jericho watched Camille and Hannah browse the racks, talking quietly as they sorted through the items. Camille held a blouse up to her chest, then looked at Hannah. The saleswoman shook her head and Camille put the shirt back. A pair of shorts apparently made the cut, and Camille draped them over her arm. One blouse was deemed appropriate and two others were rejected. There didn't seem to be any rhyme or reason to the process. But then, he was a man.

He couldn't believe he was actually shopping with Camille and not hating the experience. Three days ago he couldn't imagine willingly spending the day with her. When he'd seen her standing on his front porch, his one goal had been getting her out of his life. When he realized he had to let her stay, he'd been filled with resentment and anger at the imposition.

He'd been telling the truth when he said she wasn't as bad as he'd imagined. Years of anger had morphed her into the worst of the worst in his mind. Now he was realizing she was simply a woman trying to make it through the day the best way she could. And wasn't he doing the same? He was surprised to discover that under that rigid exterior was a woman who was not all that unpleasant. She wasn't someone he would ever like or want for a friend, but he didn't exactly hate her anymore.

He spotted a couple of chairs beside the window and took a seat. If Camille was like every other woman in the world, this could take quite a while. Settling in for the duration, he sorted through the fashion magazines on the coffee table and snagged the latest edition of the *Sweet Briar Herald.* But instead of opening the paper and catching up on the local news, he stared out the window. The sun was bright, but not enough to hurt his eyes. He leaned back and decided to indulge in a little people watching. On the rare occasions he came to town, he grabbed what he needed and beat it back to the ranch, avoiding as many people as he could.

The streets filled up with tourists who were sightseeing and purchasing souvenirs. Sweet Briar had become a popular vacation destination over the past years. Jericho had mixed feelings about the influx of people, but he knew the town had needed to adapt or risk fading away.

The bell above the door tinkled as a woman and two

teenage girls hurried in followed by a smiling middle-aged man walking at a much more leisurely pace. The females immediately charged to the clothing racks as if on a mission. The man shook his head and smiled ruefully as he settled into the seat across from Jericho. "You got suckered in, too?"

Jericho smiled. "I wouldn't call it that."

"Neither would I, if my wife was close enough to hear me."

"Wise man," Jericho said, laughing.

Hannah greeted the newcomers then grabbed an orange-and-red print dress that she took to Camille. Camille's eyes lit up as she reached for the garment. She held it in front of her and looked into a tall mirror, smiling from ear to ear. She glanced at the price tag, and the excitement slid from her. With one more look of longing, she handed the dress back to Hannah then took the items she'd selected and disappeared into the dressing room.

He wanted Camille to have that dress. That thought surprised him. Why did he care? She'd rejected it, he hadn't. No doubt she had countless dresses in her closet at home. But he'd seen the pleasure in her eyes as she'd looked at her reflection. The yearning. Her life was a wreck right now. She deserved something that would make her smile. Before Hannah could return the dress to the rack, he was across the room, credit card in hand.

"I'll take it. Don't tell Camille. I want it to be a surprise." After Hannah rang it up and placed it in a bag, he went out and hid it behind the seat in his truck, smiling when he thought of how happy Camille would be with his gift.

When Jericho returned, the older gentleman gave

him a thumbs-up. "Clearly you already know the secret to a happy life."

Before Jericho could reply, Camille was standing in front of him. He looked up and his jaw dropped. She looked like every man's dream in a fitted blue-green top and a pair of matching shorts that hit her mid-thigh, showcasing her toned legs. She'd exchanged her pumps for green flat sandals. On any other woman the clothes would have looked ordinary, but Camille looked like she could be gracing the covers of the fashion magazines scattered on the table. Her hazel eyes danced in her beautiful face. Even without a speck of makeup, she was drop-dead gorgeous. More than that, she was more relaxed than she'd been since she arrived.

His heart, which he'd believed had died a year ago, jumped like a dead battery being recharged. A hint of desire stirred in his gut, and he pushed it aside. Rising, he nodded goodbye to the older man, who was grinning broadly.

"I'm ready," Camille said.

They went to the counter and quickly paid for the clothes.

"Come back again," Hannah invited, handing over two shopping bags.

Camille and Jericho reached for the bags at the same time, and their hands brushed. A bolt of electricity shot through him, rekindling the desire he'd tamped down only seconds ago. Her eyes met his and sexual attraction arced between them, practically singeing the air. She inhaled, causing her breasts to rise.

"I've got it," Jericho said.

"Thanks." Camille stared at her hand as if she'd never seen it before. She appeared as dazed as he felt.

Jericho peered into the bags. One held new clothes and the other was filled with the clothes he'd lent her. "Is this all?"

"Yes."

"Camille—"

"I bought four tops, three pairs of shorts, and a skirt that I can mix and match." She raised her foot. "I also bought these shoes. That's enough. I don't want to be greedy."

He'd always believed that Camille was materialistic and selfish, but now he wasn't so sure. He'd been around her a few days and everything he discovered about her was contrary to what he thought he knew. Just who was the real Camille Parker?

They didn't speak as they loaded the bags into his truck. Seeing how little she'd purchased for herself, he was even happier that he'd bought that dress. She started to climb into the truck. They should probably return to the ranch. But just then, her stomach growled. "Sorry."

"Don't be. You're hungry. There's a diner not too far from here where we can grab a late breakfast."

Her brow wrinkled as she glanced around. "Are you sure it's safe?"

"Perfectly. Trust me."

Her hazel eyes met his. "I do."

Try as he might, he couldn't tamp down his pleasure at her words.

The smell of sausages frying and bread toasting greeted Jericho as he and Camille stepped inside Mabel's Diner. His stomach rumbled long and loud, letting him know he, too, could use some food.

A waitress greeted them with a coffeepot in one hand

and a smile on her face. The aroma of strong coffee was always a welcome one. "Party of two?"

"Yes."

The woman tilted her head toward the noisy dining room. "Grab any table. Someone will be right over."

"Thanks."

As they walked through the maze of chrome tables and red vinyl chairs, Jericho spotted familiar faces here and there. He nodded a greeting but didn't stop to talk. He bypassed a couple of empty tables and led Camille to a booth in the back where a busboy was loading dirty dishes into a gray plastic bin. The teenager dragged a damp cloth across the table and then swiped at the seats, removing any bits of food that the previous diners might have dropped. He set place mats on the table, efficiently added clean cups and saucers, nodded, and left.

Camille's eyes darted around the restaurant, taking in the families with small children and groups of laughing women. She blew out a breath, apparently satisfied that she was still safe.

She took the seat with her back to the wall. "I don't want anyone to sneak up on me."

"Okay." He sat down across from her. He grabbed the laminated menus from between the salt and pepper shakers, handed her one, then began studying his.

She placed her menu on the table without looking at it. "What's good?"

Jericho frowned as he tried to recall. "The omelets were good. So were the breakfast potatoes and sausage. And I remember the steak and eggs always hit the spot."

"You keep saying 'were.' Did they change owners or something? Are they under new management?"

"Not that I know of."

She stared at him as if trying to get a close-up and personal look at his soul. After a moment her eyes filled with compassion and sorrow. She'd figured out he hadn't been to the diner since he'd lost Jeanette. For a minute he thought she might touch his hand. Instead she lifted her menu and opened it, hiding her expression from him. Good. He didn't want her pity. He didn't want anyone's pity. He just wanted to be left alone. Or at least he thought he did. Being around Camille was making him change his thinking.

Coming here was a bad idea. He was about to stand when a waitress stepped up to their table. "Coffee?"

"I'd love some," Camille said, giving him a look that was pretty much a dare. If she could face her fear of being in public, would he eat in a room filled with people gossiping about him? Or would he turn tail and run? "I'm ready to order. How about you, Jericho?"

He nodded, up for the challenge. And he was hungry. "Ladies first."

"I'll have the steak and eggs, biscuits and gravy, breakfast potatoes, and a bowl of grits."

"That sounds pretty good. Make that two."

The waitress wrote down their orders and left.

Camille sipped her black coffee. "That's good." Her gaze shifted from him to just over his shoulder. He turned to see what had drawn her attention.

"Jericho, it is you. Several people told me they'd spotted you today. I wanted to see for myself. How are you?"

He rose and shook his friend's hand. Trent Knight was the chief of police and a good man. He'd been widowed himself, and had always respected Jericho's need for solitude. "Good. How about you?"

"No complaints."

"And Carmen?" Trent had remarried a couple of years ago.

Trent smiled. "She was right behind me. But you know her, she probably ran into a friend." He glanced around, then his face lit up. "Here she is."

Jericho turned and his heart nearly stopped. "You're pregnant."

"Seven months." Carmen rubbed her hand over her large stomach in the way pregnant women did. The way Jeanette had done.

"With twin boys," Trent added proudly.

How could they be so happy? Didn't they know what could go wrong? Jeanette had looked as healthy as Carmen did now. Then Jeanette and their baby were dead.

He felt a soft hand in his and looked at Camille, who smiled at him and gave his hand a gentle squeeze. Somehow she'd known he'd needed her support.

Jericho swallowed the pain that threatened to consume him. He wouldn't let the agonizing memories mar his friends' obvious joy. "Congratulations. To both of you."

"Thanks." Carmen looked at Camille. Jericho could practically see the wheels in her mind turning.

"Camille, this is Carmen and Trent Knight. Trent, Carmen, this is Camille. She's visiting me for a while."

"It's nice to meet both of you," Camille said. "And congratulations on your babies."

"Thanks. How long are you going to be in town?" Carmen asked.

A look of unease crossed Camille's face before she forced a smile. "It's open-ended."

Ever the observant lawman, Trent zeroed in on her response. He raised an eyebrow at Jericho, then smiled at Camille, apparently willing to let her vague answer pass. "I hope you enjoy your stay."

"If you have time, we'd love to have the two of you over for dinner one night," Carmen added, her eyes focused on Jericho's and Camille's clasped hands. He slid his hand free and shoved it into the pocket of his jeans.

Just because he'd brought Camille to town didn't mean he was ready to jump back into the social scene. More important, it didn't mean they were a couple as Carmen seemed to think. "We'll have to see."

"Good enough," Trent said. "We'll leave you to your meal."

Jericho dropped into his seat and exhaled.

"I'm sorry," Camille said softly.

His head snapped up. Camille's eyes looked damp, and she was blinking like mad. "For what?"

"For everything. For showing up out of nowhere and barging into your life. For not having clothes and putting you in a situation where you had to come to town. For not thinking before taking your hand and giving your friends the wrong impression. I probably have a few more things to apologize for, but I can't remember them off the top of my head. But I'm sorry for them, too."

He didn't have a clue how to respond. Sure, he hadn't been glad to see her. Given their past, that was understandable. But truth be told, he hadn't minded taking her shopping. And he was looking forward to eating the breakfast he'd just ordered. He might not have wanted to interact with his old friends yet, but if he had to, Trent and Carmen were the ones he would have chosen.

And perhaps it wasn't a bad thing that they'd run into Trent just now. Maybe they should have let the chief know about Camille's problem. Jericho still believed she was perfectly safe in Sweet Briar, but he was a rancher, not a cop. Camille's life was at stake, so maybe they should consult a professional.

"You don't need to apologize."

"Really?" The hope in her voice surprised him. She really seemed to be worried that she'd hurt him in some way. He was going to have to reconsider everything he thought he knew about her. She might not be the person he'd believed her to be for the past five years.

"Really." The waitress returned with their food. "Now let's eat."

After quickly stopping at a Western wear shop and buying two pairs of jeans, a pair of boots that Camille would no doubt toss into the back of her closet when she returned to New York, and a dove-gray felt cowboy hat Jericho insisted she needed to keep the sun out of her eyes, they headed for a grocery store to stock up on food. Camille's eyebrows rose when they pulled into the parking lot of the surprisingly large store. "I didn't expect to see a supermarket this big in a small town."

"Why not? People need food wherever they live. The store may not carry everything you're used to in New York, but they stock a nice variety."

They grabbed a cart and began browsing the aisles. Camille took a few steps and began filling the cart. When she used to cook on Saturdays, she'd planned her menu carefully and made her list accordingly. She didn't have a list today, but she didn't need one. She'd been in Jericho's home for a few days and knew he needed everything.

Jericho was quiet as he walked beside her. He occasionally added something to the cart, but for the most part allowed her to choose the items and brands she preferred. After about twenty minutes, his silence began to unnerve her. She held up a jar of peanut butter. "Do you like this brand?"

Jericho looked at her, his face ravaged with agony. She forgot about the peanut butter and put her hand on his arm. "What's wrong?"

He turned away as if to hide his expression from her. His shoulders lifted and then fell. "The last time I was in here was with Jeanette. Two days before. She was so excited about the baby. He'd been moving around more. She looked so healthy."

"Do you want to leave? Maybe wait in the truck? I don't mind shopping alone." They'd been in town for a couple of hours, and she believed she would be safe in the store without him.

"No. I need to do this. I can't keep driving to Willow Creek for food. Being here with you is actually helping." He placed a hand over hers, and she wished she could turn hers over so they were holding hands. When he looked at her, his eyes were free of the pain that had been there moments earlier, although the shadows were still there.

Her heart leaped at his words, and her skin tingled under his touch. She'd expected the physical reaction because she'd experienced it before, but she was surprised to be warmed by his words.

Jericho was good-looking. But she was becoming attracted to the man behind the gorgeous face and muscular body. She didn't understand how it was possible to go from hating him to being attracted in under a week. It didn't make sense.

But then nothing in her life made sense right now.

They finished shopping, filling the cart to overflowing, then checked out. As they drove back to the Double J, they talked quietly, the tension that had been present in their previous interactions blessedly absent.

Chapter Six

Camille crept down the stairs, Shadow beside her. The dog had taken to sleeping outside her door. When he wasn't chasing squirrels and rabbits, he followed her around like, well, a shadow. The third step creaked and Camille held her breath, hoping she hadn't awakened Jericho. He'd been so generous yesterday, she was determined to repay his kindness by preparing him a substantial breakfast before he started work. His work was physical and she wanted to make sure he had the fuel he needed.

She let Shadow outside to run around for a while, then set to work. Cooking was something she loved, and she soon lost track of time.

"Something smells good."

Camille looked up from the stove and returned Jericho's smile with one of her own. Dressed in a black cotton shirt and relaxed jeans, he seemed perfectly at ease and comfortable with himself.

She wondered how he pulled that off. Not that she was uncomfortable with herself exactly. It just seemed like she was always striving to reach that elusive goal that would mean she'd finally made it. To finally have the proof that she was good enough. She hated always looking over her shoulder to see who was gaining on her. She didn't like thinking there was only one brass ring in the world and she had to be the one to grab it and hold on to it at all costs.

"Is something wrong?"

"No. Why do you ask?" Camille blinked and tried to regain her tranquility.

"You had the saddest expression on your face."

She shook her head, then turned back to the pan and flipped over the sausage. All this time on her hands was giving her too much room to think. Not that she was against introspection. She just was unsure about what she was going to do with the information she unearthed. What did all this self-awareness matter if she wasn't in a position to change who she was?

"I'm fine. Just thinking about my situation." Not the killers after her, but the rest of her life, which she was discovering was a mess. "I'd rather not talk about it. I'd like to have a few minutes where I could pretend all was good."

"Okay." Jericho raised the top of the waffle iron and lifted out the golden waffles and placed them on a plate. He expertly spread butter across them before adding more batter.

"I didn't think you could cook."

"Didn't see much point in cooking just for myself."

"You must miss Jeanette."

"Yes."

He didn't elaborate. He didn't need to. That one whispered word spoke more powerfully of how painful his life had been since Jeanette's death than an entire speech. That one word described grief so deep it was physical. Emptiness so wide the entire house groaned with it.

Knowing nothing she could say would ease his pain, she didn't try. Instead, she nodded, signaling her understanding. The quiet lasted until they'd nearly finished eating breakfast. Although it had started out filled with sorrow, it had eased into a companionable silence.

But Camille craved conversation. She ate without talking at home, the only voices those on her television set or the radio. Having another person around, even Jericho, was a treat.

"Is it hard to take care of horses?" Although she'd simply been searching for an easy topic, she realized she wanted to know. "They're so big. I hate to admit it, but up close, they seem a little bit scary."

He chewed a piece of sausage, taking his time before answering. "I'm not sure what you mean by *hard*. It takes work. Like any other animal, horses need to be fed. They also need exercise. Brushing. Things like that." He swallowed the last of his coffee and rose. "Speaking of which, I'd better get out there. Thanks for making breakfast. I'd remind you that you don't have to cook for me, but I like your cooking just a little too much."

He reached for his plate, and she stopped him with a hand on his. "I'll take care of the dishes. You have animals waiting for you."

He turned back when he reached the door. "If you want, you can come meet the horses. You'll see that they're nothing to be afraid of."

She hesitated. She needed to overcome her fear, but jumping in with both feet seemed a little rash. Maybe she could look at them from a distance.

She couldn't believe herself. When had she become so timid? Besides, Jericho would be there. Not that she would need him. She was strong. "Sure. When's good?"

"Give me a couple hours."

"How's ten sound?"

"Perfect." He put on his cowboy hat, then opened the door. She couldn't be certain, but she thought she heard him whistling as he left. The joy in that sound was contagious, and although she didn't know how to whistle, she could hum. So she did.

"I know, I'm late," Jericho said as he reached the storage bin. He grabbed the measuring cup and bucket so he could begin filling the troughs. Buttercup snorted and knocked her head against his shoulder. He gave her a pat on her neck, then moved on to the next stall. As he fed Sundance, he could hear Diablo stomping his foot against the floor, clearly displeased at being kept waiting to eat.

When he reached Diablo's stall, he measured and poured grain for his favorite horse, then leaned against the wall. "You wouldn't be so grumpy if you knew what happened. It would have been rude of me to skip breakfast after Camille went to so much trouble to cook for me." Not that good manners and food were the only things that kept him in the kitchen.

He frowned, not liking that thought at all. Jeanette

had been his wife. She'd been the only woman who could make him lose track of time. The only woman capable of making him forget there had been a world apart from the two of them. He'd loved her completely. He still did. There was no room for Camille or any other woman in his life, much less his heart.

The stallion didn't look up from his food. Jericho locked the stall to let him eat in peace while he wrestled with his conflicted feelings. When the horses had finished eating, he led them into the corral, then started cleaning the stalls. He was putting away the shovel and wheelbarrow when he heard footsteps. He turned as Camille approached. She'd dressed in a simple top that emphasized her tiny waist and her new jeans and boots that showcased her mile-long legs. Although the clothes were no different from those worn by hundreds of other women, they somehow looked sexier and more appealing on her. Her hips swayed seductively as she grew nearer, and desire exploded through him like a grenade. He exhaled as he struggled to gain control of his body.

He tried reminding himself that a pretty outside didn't always make for a pretty inside, but he wasn't as successful today as he'd been in the past. Now that he'd spent time with Camille, he was discovering she wasn't ugly inside. Not that it mattered. He wasn't interested. He couldn't allow himself to be.

"Where are the horses?" she asked, a quizzical smile on her face.

"In the corral. I needed to clean the stalls."

"Do you need help?"

Camille Parker was actually volunteering to sweep horse crap? No way. She probably had no idea what was involved. She was a city girl, after all. "No. I'm done. Come on."

She walked beside him. Her legs were nearly as long as his, so he didn't need to shorten his stride. As they neared the horses, Camille moved so close to him her shoulder bumped his and their thighs brushed. Her sweet scent mingled with the smell of fresh grass. The combination was heady and more appealing than anything he had smelled in the longest time. His body reacted instantly; he needed to get lasting control and not just another five-second fix.

He took a few more steps before he realized she was no longer beside him. Camille was frozen some feet away, her eyes focused on the corral.

"What's wrong?"

"Nothing. I'm just not so sure this is a good idea."

He could spend the next hour talking to her, trying to convince her she had nothing to fear, or he could just show her how gentle his horses were. People used to come from three states to have him work with their horses. He'd never met one he couldn't tame. His were the best of the best.

She turned her turbulent eyes to his. "I know someone who was bitten by a horse."

"Really?"

"Yes. In high school. One of my classmates was bitten on the thigh. She showed me the bruise. It was gigantic. I've never seen anything like it. I can't imagine how much that hurt, but it had to be a lot."

Jericho nodded slowly, rubbing his chin. "Horses have been known to bite, but not mine. My horses are well trained and docile. I'd never put you in danger."

"I know. Still…" She looked at the horse's enormous teeth and shuddered.

"Ingrained fears can take time to overcome. There's no pressure. I thought you would enjoy riding to sort of kill time." He winced. "Sorry. Poor choice of words."

"It's not like I've forgotten why I'm here. The fear is always with me. Sometimes it's only a low hum and at other times it's a shriek. But I'm always aware of my situation. I'm always scared."

Her confession surprised him. He didn't expect her to be that open with him. "Are you scared right now?"

"Yes. The fear is more like a whisper, but still, it's there."

"That's no way to live. Do you have any idea how much longer the investigation will last?"

"Not really. Agent Delgado said things would start to speed up. Then he had the accident."

"A case this big will make the news. We should start checking the internet for information every day."

"I will."

She looked so miserable he had to do something to help. "Wait here."

He hopped over the fence, walked up to Buttercup. He rubbed his hand down her neck, well aware that Camille was watching his every move. The horse nickered, and Camille jumped. Jericho grabbed the horse's halter and led her to the fence. "You don't have to be afraid. Buttercup is as gentle as they come. She loves people."

Camille stood still, yet he could practically see the wheels whirling in her head as she debated internally. Finally she stiffened her spine, lifted her chin and took a determined step in his direction. Just as he expected, her pride wouldn't let her turn tail and run, at least not with him there as a witness. If he hadn't been watching closely he might have missed the way her hands trembled before she shoved them into her pockets. He admired the way she was facing her fears.

She reached the fence and leaned against it. When she looked up, her eyes were filled with trust. His heart stumbled at her faith in him. But hadn't she shown that same trust when she'd arrived on his doorstep? Despite the previous bad blood between them, she'd believed in her heart that he would protect her.

Of course he would. He wasn't the type of man who would turn his back on anyone in need, even if that person had previously been the one and only name on his enemy list. But he hadn't expected Camille to know that. Yet she had. Later he would think about what, if anything, that meant. For now, he needed to help her overcome her fear of horses.

"Just relax. You're perfectly safe."

Camille gave a shadow of her luminous smile.

"Buttercup likes when you pat the side of her neck." He demonstrated, brushing his hand over the horse.

Camille reached over the fence as if she were putting her hand in a box of snakes and touched Buttercup with the tips of her fingers. Her eyes lit up, and she gasped. "She's so soft."

"Yes."

She smoothed her entire hand over Buttercup's neck in a gentle caress. He wondered how her hands would feel on his bare chest before he banished the disloyal thought. Jeanette had been his one and only. He would never be unfaithful to her. Especially with Camille. She was the absolute worst person in the world for him. His mind knew that, so why didn't his body?

"Now what should I do?" she asked, dragging him back to the present.

"You can keep patting her on the neck. She really likes that."

Camille stroked the horse with more confidence, and this time her smile was bright. "What about carrots and sugar cubes? Is it true they like to eat them, or is that an old wives' tale?"

"It's true. And I just happen to have a few with me."

He took a carrot from his shirt pocket. Although he could have told Camille how to hold her hand to safely feed Buttercup, he didn't. Instead he took her hand in his, marveling at just how small and soft it was. She didn't resist when he turned her hand over, palm up, and placed the carrot there. "Always keep your fingers flat."

Buttercup lowered her head and took the treat, her lips moving over Camille's hand.

"That tickles," Camille said and dissolved into giggles. She sounded so much like a young girl that Jericho had a hard time remembering she was a financial big shot. The carefree sound transported Jericho back to happier times when the ranch was filled with laughter and joy. Love. He'd been happy, loving every minute of his days. Lately he'd just been trying to get from sunrise to sunset. Oddly enough, he hadn't felt that way today.

"This is fun."

"Do you want me to saddle her for you?"

Camille backed away with her hands upraised. "Not yet." She looked down at her feet as if unable to meet his eyes and brushed at her jeans. "I know you must think I'm stupid or chicken."

He nudged her shoulder. "Nah, City Girl. You've seen

evidence of what a horse can do. I'm proud of you for even touching Buttercup and letting her eat from your hand. That's a big step."

Camille felt warm all over at Jericho's compliment. She knew it was sincere, which made it even more precious. But the warmth was quickly followed by discomfort. Why did his opinion of her matter so much? She hadn't thought about him in years. But now she was literally running for her life and he was protecting her. Jericho was the only thing standing between her and a killer. Maybe that's why she was starting to see him differently. Why she was suddenly finding him more attractive. But this wasn't real life. The killers would be caught and she would return to New York. Once things went back to normal, these insane feelings would surely vanish.

She took refuge in small talk. "How many horses do you have?"

"Eleven."

"Do you offer horseback rides?"

"You mean like a business for tourists?"

She nodded.

"No. I breed horses. My horses are docile enough for even the most inexperienced riders, of course." He rubbed Buttercup's neck again.

"Do you breed them to race?"

"No. Midnight has great lines and I'd dreamed of it once. But that was before."

Before Jeanette died.

He looked over the fields, lost in his thoughts. She knew he wasn't seeing the acres of rolling green hills surrounding them. Perhaps he was visualizing the past when Jeanette was alive and his life was wonderful.

She sensed he needed to be alone. She could do with a little distance herself. "Thanks for introducing me to your horses."

His smile was just a faint replica of the one he'd bestowed upon her earlier. "My pleasure. You're welcome to come around anytime."

"Thanks." She stepped away, then turned back. "If it's okay with you, I'd like to work in the garden. It's kind of overrun with weeds and could use some pruning."

"Getting antsy?"

"Sort of. Being busy will help keep my scary thoughts under control." In theory, at least. "I'd enjoy it."

"I'll get the tools for you."

She watched as he went. Maybe a few hours digging in the dirt would be what she needed to straighten out her tangled emotions.

Chapter Seven

Camille stood at the kitchen sink, scrubbing her hands. She'd broken two nails while gardening, but she didn't mind. Digging in the soil may have ruined her manicure, but it had soothed her soul and relaxed her spirit. There was still a long way to go before the garden was restored to its former glory, but she'd made substantial progress. She'd trimmed shrubs and pulled countless weeds. Jericho had found a bag of fertilizer, and she'd spread that. When she was finished he'd have a pretty view right outside his window.

Moving the curtain aside, she peered out the window. The stable was visible and she could see Jericho as he strode through the barn door, moving as confidently as ever. He crossed the grass, Shadow barking and running in circles around him. Jericho's gait was easy, and his long legs ate up the ground. His chest was broad and muscular, but not the unnatural size of men who lifted weights in public and swallowed steroids in secret. His physique was the result of hard work. Not an inch of fat lay beneath his blue chambray shirt. When she'd first arrived, she'd thought he was too thin. Now she knew better.

Her eyes traveled to his face. She'd never found pretty boys appealing, and that hadn't changed. Jericho had strong features that reflected his inner strength. His jaw was square with a five o'clock shadow beginning to make an appearance. His dark eyes were intelligent, and his lips were just full enough to make her wonder what they would feel like pressed against hers in a real kiss. Or skimming over her body. She forced the thought away before it could take root in her heart. He wasn't interested in her in that way. And she certainly shouldn't think of him that way either.

She dried her hands and moved away from the window as he stepped into the kitchen.

"Sorry I'm late. I wanted to get in here earlier to help you, but one of the horses had a bit of trouble settling down."

He looked from her to the table. She'd picked a bunch of yellow and purple flowers and arranged them in a vase, creating a simple centerpiece.

He brushed a finger over a purple blossom. "Fancy. Give me a few minutes to shower and put on clean clothes."

After he left she looked at her own clothes, wishing she had on something other than her denim shorts and pale yellow tank top. There was no way she could change now, though. That would be too obvious. Besides, what would she change into? Her entire wardrobe consisted of clothes like these.

She rushed to the powder room and studied her reflection in the mirror. Her shoulder-length black hair looked as good as could be expected considering she'd missed her regularly scheduled salon appointment and didn't have any of her styling tools. She ran a hand through it, taming her natural waves. Her eyes were clear and bright. She didn't have any makeup with her, and purchasing it had been out of the question. It wasn't a necessity. Fortunately, time in the sun had given her skin a nice glow. All things considered, she looked okay.

Returning to the kitchen, she stirred the cheddar and broccoli soup, then ladled it into bowls to cool.

"Something smells absolutely amazing."

Jericho crossed the room and didn't stop until he was beside her. Her heart stuttered at his nearness, and goose bumps popped up on her arms. She inhaled and got a whiff of soap and clean male.

"Thanks."

Jericho was dressed in black jeans that revealed his muscular thighs and a T-shirt that pulled against his broad chest. Camille's mouth began to water, and it had nothing to do with the grilled pork chops.

This was insane. She barely liked the man. Okay, so he wasn't a horrible person, but that didn't make him a potential romantic interest. She needed to stop this ridiculous attraction before it got her heart in trouble.

He lifted one side of his mouth in that sexy half smile that threatened to decimate her good sense. "I know I'm late to the party, but is there anything I can do to help?"

She put the mashed potatoes on the table, then

brushed her hands against her shorts. "No. Everything is done. All that's left to do is the eating."

He pulled out her chair and she murmured her thanks, pleased by the courtesy.

"This is delicious," he said after sampling everything. "My friend Brandon is the chef who drops off food from time to time. This is just as good as what he makes."

Ah, so the chef friend was a guy. Not that it mattered. The important thing was that Jericho had a friend who cared enough about him to keep him from starving.

"He owns a restaurant in town," Jericho added.

"Is he the same guy who's getting married?"

"How do you know that?"

"Hannah mentioned it. She designed the dresses for the bridesmaids."

"Yes." Jericho rubbed a hand across his forehead and frowned. "Brandon is one of my best friends and I barely talk to him. I've been so wrapped up in my own life I haven't considered what's been happening with my friends."

"You've been mourning. You lost a wife and a child. Your friends understand."

He stared at her so long she wondered if she had food stuck in her teeth. Or maybe she'd said the wrong thing by mentioning Jeanette. "What?"

"I've been thinking about your situation and what we should do."

She frowned and her heart sped up. "I've been trying not to think of it."

"Using the old ostrich-with-her-head-in-the-sand approach to problem solving."

"It gets me through the day."

"I think we should let Trent know what's going on."

She dropped her fork and knife, her hunger forgotten. "No. He might do something to draw them here. Since I don't even know who I'm hiding from, they could walk right up to me and I'd never know." She shot to her feet. "Maybe staying in Sweet Briar is a mistake. I should keep moving. A moving target is harder to hit."

He stood and took her hand before she could escape. Of course, she had no idea where she could run. Her reasons for coming here hadn't changed. Jericho was still her only hope.

"Shh. I didn't mean to upset you. Please sit back down. It was just a suggestion. If you say no, the answer is no. I won't say a thing to Trent or anyone else. But I think we need to at least discuss it before you reject the idea."

"My life is the one on the line here, so the final decision has to be mine."

"By coming here you put my life at risk, too. Isn't that one of the reasons you chose me? Because you didn't want to put someone you love in danger?"

Shame swamped her. Sure, she knew this was the last place anyone would think to look, but that was only part of it. If she had to risk someone's life, she preferred it be someone she hated. Except she didn't hate him now. "Sorry."

He shrugged. "I'm not looking for an apology. I just want you to know that I have something at stake, too. You're not alone."

She was glad of that, even if she didn't like what he was proposing.

"But we need a way to find out how the investigation is going. You can't hide out here forever."

Of course she couldn't. He was probably counting the minutes until he would be rid of her. He might be treating her with kindness, but the fact remained that they weren't friends. Even if they no longer actively hated each other, that didn't mean he wanted her to live with him indefinitely. And she did have a life to get back to. A job. Family and friends.

"I know."

"Just think about it. We don't have to decide anything now, but we need to come up with a plan. Right now I can't think of a better one."

Neither could she. She knew Jericho trusted Trent, but could she?

He gave her hand a gentle squeeze, which despite her jangling nerves sent sparks shooting throughout her body. Apparently even fear of discovery couldn't dampen the fires he lit in her. "Stop worrying, Camille. We'll figure this out."

She managed a wobbly smile. "I don't have much of an appetite anymore."

"How about a walk? There's still a bit of daylight left."

"That would be nice."

He kept hold of her hand as he led her out the back door, and it felt perfectly natural. His palm was calloused yet warm against hers. She could have asked him why he'd taken her hand, but decided not to overthink things. He probably wasn't even aware of what he'd done.

"Which way did you go on your walk the other day?"

She pointed north. At least she thought it was north. "Toward the road."

"Then let's go in a different direction. There's a

stream about a mile from here. Do you think you can make it?"

He looked so serious she smiled. "Yes."

The evening was perfect and a gentle breeze blew, rustling the leaves in the giant trees. Birds flew overhead while others chirped from the safety of their nests. The farther away from the house they got, the more distant her problems seemed. She was finally able to breathe again.

Two squirrels ran down one tree, scampered across the grass and then ran up another tree. Perhaps they'd sneaked out and their mother was on the way home. She sighed at the fanciful image.

"Penny for your thoughts."

She shook her head. She didn't know how she'd handle it if he laughed at her.

"Come on." His brown eyes twinkled and then grew serious. "You can tell me. I promise not to make fun of you."

Darn her insecurity. Why did she care what he thought? He was just a man. She'd be out of here soon and likely wouldn't see him again.

But suddenly she wasn't so anxious to get back to New York. Here she was able to slow down long enough to hear herself think. She even had time to cook, which she absolutely loved. The stars that filled the night sky were brighter here, and the peaceful evening was so different from the constant bustle of the city.

She sighed. It mattered because he mattered. There. She admitted it. She wanted him to think well of her. But she was a grown woman. Not some girl who couldn't share a random thought even if it revealed a part of herself that she preferred stay hidden.

"I saw the way the squirrels ran from tree to tree and imagined they were trying to get home before they got caught sneaking out."

"That's funny." One corner of his mouth lifted in a smile. "That wasn't so bad, was it?"

"What?"

"Sharing a personal thought."

"I wouldn't say it was easy, but I got through it."

"It gets easier with practice."

"I'll take your word for it."

He laughed and nudged her with his shoulder, and she found herself laughing, too. His charm was lethal.

They walked in silence for a few minutes more before Jericho stopped.

Camille looked around in awe. The entire ranch was beautiful, but this spot was exceptionally so. She turned in a slow circle. No matter which direction she looked, she saw nature at its most spectacular. The grass was greener than the small patches of lawn in New York. And more fragrant. "This is wonderful."

"Come on, we're almost to the stream."

They climbed up a small hill. Soon a new sound joined the others. A moment later they were at the water. The stream bubbled over rocks as it wound its way out of sight. The setting sun made the water look like liquid diamonds.

Jericho guided her to a boulder where they sat side by side. His broad shoulder brushed against hers, and sparks seemed to shoot between them. He didn't appear to notice. The attraction was definitely one-sided. But then she already knew that. His mind was too filled with Jeanette to even think of another woman.

"I come here when I need to escape my thoughts. I

don't always get the peace I'm searching for, but I have a better chance here than anywhere else."

"I can imagine anything would be possible here." There was nothing but rolling hills and leafy trees as far as the eye could see. Man had yet to interfere with the pristine quality of the land. She closed her eyes and breathed deeply, inhaling the fresh air and exhaling a lifetime of tension.

"Look," Jericho whispered in her ear. His breath brushed against the sensitive skin beneath her ear, stirring feelings of intense longing in her. She shivered, although the evening was warm.

"Where?" Camille whispered in return. She opened her eyes and peered into his. He was so close that if she moved even an inch their lips would touch.

"There." He pointed.

"Oh," she turned and gasped. A mother deer and her two babies were emerging from the shadows and approaching the stream. First the mother drank and then the two fawns. Camille glanced over at Jericho. He wasn't looking at the deer but at her. He was so close she could see tiny flecks of gold in his brown eyes. Her excitement at the wonders of nature morphed into a different type of excitement, and her skin tingled with anticipation. They sat in frozen silence. A flock of birds flew overhead. Jericho blinked and turned away, breaking the spell.

What the hell? Why had he brought Camille here? He could tell himself he wanted to soothe her fears after she'd gotten so worked up. Perhaps that was true. But that wasn't the entire reason. Crazy as it sounded, he wanted to share a place that had meaning for him. He wanted to see her reaction. He needed to know if a city girl like her could appreciate the simple beauty of the ranch. And, boy, had she. The expression on her face could only be described as pure bliss. She'd practically vibrated with joy when she'd seen the deer.

Camille was still sitting very close to him, her unique scent tempting him to pull her even closer. He wouldn't, though. He needed to maintain distance between them. Her life was in turmoil. The last thing she needed was for him to act on his confusing feelings and make her life even more tumultuous.

There was no doubt he was confused. Until she showed up on his doorstep, his feelings for her had been perfectly clear. Now his certainty was starting to blur. The kind and thoughtful Camille he was discovering was completely different from the Camille of five years ago.

But no matter how different she appeared, he wasn't going to become enthralled by this woman. His attraction couldn't be real. They were too different. They had totally different outlooks on life. The amount of time they were spending together had to be to blame for this insanity. Add in the air of danger—even though she was perfectly safe here—and his senses were naturally heightened. Every feeling was more intense than it would have been under ordinary circumstances.

He'd been alone for over a year, interacting with others only when necessary. He could count on one hand the number of times he'd shared a meal with someone in the past year. And those occasions had always been when Brandon barged in. Given how solitary his existence had been, his responses were normal. He would react to any woman under these circumstances. There was nothing special about Camille Parker. Nothing at all.

"I could stay here forever," Camille said. She wrapped her arms around her knees, then turned and smiled at him.

She was so beautiful. His heart thudded in his chest, and all he could do was stare at her. When he didn't respond, her smiled faded. "Not that I have designs on the Double J. I know you probably regret letting me in your door."

Her pained laugh reached inside and squeezed his heart. His silence had hurt her. "Not at all."

But his answer had come too late. Her joy had faded. They sat in stilted silence for a while before she stood and shoved her hands in her pockets. "I guess we should be getting back."

He rose, as well. The distance was back between them. He told himself it was for the best and that he preferred it this way, but he knew he'd told himself a whopper of a lie. Somehow he had to find a way to face the truth.

Chapter Eight

Jericho heard the sound of Camille's boots tapping on the stable floor, and despite himself his heart began to race. The walk back to the house last night had been awkward. He'd wanted to avoid an equally awkward breakfast, so he'd grabbed a piece of toast and a mug of coffee, claiming he had a lot of work to do. That was wrong. It wasn't fair to avoid her. She wasn't to blame for his mixed-up feelings. It wasn't her fault that he was becoming attracted to her no matter how hard he fought against it. And Camille was making an effort to get along. Courtesy demanded that he do the same.

He turned and waited for her to reach him.

She smiled as if the awkwardness between them didn't exist. "I'm here to help."

He wasn't expecting that. "Are you? And just what do you propose to do?"

She shrugged and her sweet scent wafted in the air, making him wish for something he had long since given up on. "Whatever you need. I guess I could rake out the old hay."

"Do you have any idea what's in that old hay, City Girl?" He doubted it. He didn't want to be within screaming distance when she figured it out.

"Not for sure, but I can take a wild guess. I don't imagine stalls come equipped with toilets, and I don't see a litter box."

And she was willing to clean it up? Jeanette had loved living and working on the ranch, but she'd drawn the line at cleaning up after the animals. He'd assumed Camille would do the same. Maybe it was time to stop assuming he knew her and let her show him who she was.

"All right, then. I'd appreciate the help. You need gloves so you won't end up with calluses."

For a while he'd employed teenage brothers from a neighboring ranch as hands, so he had plenty of leather gloves. He grabbed a tan pair that looked about her size and offered them to her. Her hazel eyes sparkled as if she was about to have the time of her life scooping up horse crap. Dressed in jeans and a T-shirt, and absolutely no makeup, she should have looked plain. Instead she was ravishing. Her skin was free of blemishes, and she seemed to glow from within. Her cheekbones were high in her perfect face. Her full lips, parted in excitement, were all too kissable.

His body jumped to attention, reminding him that he was still a man. A man who had been without a woman for over a year. Until Camille's arrival, he hadn't cared. His desires had been dormant, and sex was the furthest thing from his mind. Now his body was wide awake and jumping up and down demanding attention. He focused on trying to shut down his libido, but he'd have to work until he dropped to have a chance of lulling his desires back to sleep.

Camille slipped her hands into the gloves, then brushed them over her slender thighs. "I'm ready."

So was he. Too bad they weren't talking about the same thing.

He grabbed the tools and led her to the first stall. The horses were in the pasture, so the stall was empty.

"Last chance to change your mind."

She lifted her cute little nose in the air. "I won't dignify that with a response."

He chuckled and called to her over his shoulder as he walked away. "Hate to tell you this, City Girl, but that was a response."

He started on the stall across from her. He expected Camille to work slowly. To his surprise, she finished a few seconds after he did.

He must have looked as surprised as he felt because she laughed. "What's the matter, Country Boy? Surprised that a city girl can keep up with you?"

A laugh burst out of him. "I have no response."

"I hate to tell you this, but that was a response."

Shaking his head, he grabbed the handles of his full wheelbarrow and headed for the door. She did the same, following him until they reached the pile where they emptied their loads. He hid his admiration as they returned to the barn to clean more stalls.

He could hear Camille singing popular songs as she worked, making up words when she didn't know the right ones. She had a nice voice and managed to stay on key for the most part. He'd cleaned more stalls than he could count in his life, and he had yet to sing while doing so. Camille was definitely an original.

Camille leaned against the wall of the last stall and wiped her forearm across her forehead. She was tired but exhilarated. The job was quite physical and she'd used muscles she hadn't known she had, which accounted for her exhaustion. It was Jericho's presence that made her feel like bubbles in champagne. As they worked, they'd traded jokes, Jericho's corny and hers only slightly less so. They'd laughed, and she'd enjoyed herself immensely. Now they were finished and Jericho was putting away the tools.

While they had been cleaning the stalls and laying down fresh hay, she'd reached a decision. She was going to confront her fear of horses. She was twenty-seven years old, much too old to let childish fears rule her life. Millions of people rode horses every day without incident. Her classmate being bitten was an aberration, just as Jericho said.

She looked up and found Jericho staring at her. She must look a mess. Her T-shirt was sweaty and clinging to her torso. Several strands of hair had escaped her ponytail, and she'd long since stopped brushing them behind her ears. Suddenly self-conscious, she wished she didn't look like she'd been mucking out stalls. Or worse, that she didn't smell like it.

Of course, the hard work looked fabulous on him. His shirt was also clinging to him, but it only emphasized his muscular chest and six-pack abs. Rather than smelling bad, his masculine scent was intoxicating.

He smiled and her heart skipped a beat. "I'm impressed. Thanks for your help."

His words warmed her, and she grinned so broadly you'd think she'd never received a compliment before. "You're welcome."

She walked beside him down the center aisle and out the double doors. The sun was shining brightly in the blue sky. A gentle breeze blew and she pulled her T-shirt away from her chest, allowing the breeze to cool her. Several rabbits were nibbling on grass as if they were in a restaurant. They didn't even look up as she and Jericho passed. Apparently they weren't concerned about being featured on the dinner menu.

"Rabbits aren't the smartest animals in the kingdom," Jericho said, laughing and shaking his head.

"Clearly." They were getting closer to the corrals. With each step, the horses loomed larger. When they got there, Jericho leaned against the top rail of the fence and hooked a foot on the bottom rail. She did the same.

She took a deep breath. It was now or never. "I want to ride."

He pushed back his hat and stared at her, approval in his eyes. "What brought this about?"

"It just seems ridiculous to be afraid, especially since I'm on a ranch."

"Okay. I'll saddle up Buttercup for you before you change your mind."

He might have been jesting, but doubt was already beginning to rear its ugly head. She punched it in the nose. She'd blown the whistle on criminals. Surely she could sit on a horse.

It was too late to worry about it. Jericho had already

saddled Buttercup and was leading her to Camille, the clip-clop of hooves growing louder.

Faking courage she didn't come close to feeling, Camille stepped up to the tall horse. Little children rode horses every day. She was at least as brave as a seven-year-old. "What should I do?"

"Take a deep breath and blow it out."

She complied. "Now what?"

"You're going to get on."

She looked from the horse to him and back. Even at her height, she didn't see how she would pull off that feat without either hurting or embarrassing herself. Neither option held appeal. "How?"

"Come over here."

He was standing on Buttercup's left side. Camille cautiously moved up beside him.

"Put your left foot in the stirrup and hold on to the saddle horn to pull yourself up. I'll hold the reins. Swing your right leg over. Okay? That's all there is to it." He gestured as he spoke, pointing out the stirrup and saddle horn.

Okay? "Easy peasy." *Not.*

"Take your time. Neither Buttercup nor I am in a hurry."

"I'm ready." She forced herself to put her foot into the stirrup and grabbed hold of the saddle. She hopped a couple of times but couldn't get high enough to swing her right leg over the horse. Jericho grabbed her around her waist and lifted her. In a movement that was anything but graceful, she swung her leg over the back of the horse and dropped into the saddle. She knew a moment of exhilaration. She was sitting on a horse!

She looked down. *Whoa.* She was sitting on a horse.

It was a lot higher than she'd thought. Why hadn't she asked how to get off *before* she got on?

The horse took a couple of small steps, and panic bloomed in her stomach. "This is so not a good idea."

"It's fine." Jericho rubbed Buttercup's neck. "Take the reins so you can hold on."

She took the straps, then squeezed them in a death grip.

"Let's take a walk around the corral."

A squeal escaped her.

"Don't worry. I'm going to walk beside you."

"What if I fall?"

"I'll catch you."

He sounded so sincere her stomach settled and her fears calmed. Until the horse began to walk. The motion was unnatural, and she couldn't seem to adjust her body to it. She whimpered.

"It's okay." Before she knew what he intended, he had swung up on the horse and sat behind her. He wrapped his arms around her waist and pried the reins from her hands. "Lean against me and relax. I won't let you fall."

She wanted to move, but she couldn't. Fear had gripped her, and she couldn't shake free. Leaning forward, he spoke gently into her ear, his voice sending chills down her spine. "You're safe with me, Camille. Trust me."

She did. Exhaling, she leaned back against his hard chest. He jiggled the reins and the horse began to walk slowly. Buttercup's movements were no longer frightening. Instead, with Jericho's arms wrapped around her, it felt almost sensual. Camille let her head fall against Jericho's shoulder.

"See, it's not so scary."

Riding the horse wasn't scary. It was actually kind of nice. Feeling so safe and comfortable in Jericho's arms? That was terrifying.

Chapter Nine

Camille rose from the table stiffly, trying and failing to stifle a groan. Every part of her body ached, including her hair. Jericho had warned her about overdoing it her first day, but she'd been too excited to listen. Now she wished she hadn't been so stubborn. After she'd grown comfortable on Buttercup, she'd begged to do some real riding. Jericho had suggested they wait until tomorrow, but she had been exhilarated and didn't want to stop. Besides, she didn't want to risk letting her fear return. Jericho had reluctantly saddled Diablo and taken her on a ride around the ranch.

The hour had been thrilling for more reasons than one. Jericho's nearness had set her imagination free, and she'd pictured herself riding off into the sunset with him. He had been striking, riding his stallion with such confidence. Sitting tall in the saddle, his muscular legs steering the horse with practiced ease, his eyes shaded from the sun by the brim of his Western hat, he put all other men to shame.

"Let me take your plate."

She slid back into her chair. "Thanks. I guess I should have listened to you."

"You think?" He suddenly seemed angry, as if he was the one suffering.

"I just thought since I'm in pretty good shape I would be all right."

"Riding a horse isn't like riding a bike."

He'd get no argument there. She just wished he'd stop frowning at her. She shifted, trying to find a way to sit comfortably on her aching backside. There wasn't one. "Yeah. I get that now."

He stared at her a long moment and then huffed out a breath. "You need to soak in the tub."

"Good idea." She pushed back her chair, and he was immediately beside her, helping her to her feet. He wrapped his arm around her waist, and despite the fact that her body was screaming with misery, a flicker of desire stirred up butterflies in her stomach. The pain didn't stop the yearning his touch created inside her.

She shuffled around the table and was halfway to the door when he muttered a curse under his breath. An instant later, he swept her up in his arms. Heart pounding, she couldn't speak a word of protest to save her life. And she really should protest. She was a grown woman responsible enough to suffer the consequences of her actions.

But it felt so good to be held in his arms.

He climbed the stairs, then hesitated. She thought he might be ready to put her down—after all, she was five

foot ten, not some tiny little thing—so she reluctantly
began to ease out of his arms. He tightened his hold on
her and then, as if he'd reached a conclusion of some
sort, pushed open the door to his bedroom, walking
through it to his master bath, where he gently lowered
her onto the closed toilet seat.

"My tub has jets. The one in the guest bathroom
doesn't." He backed away as if he'd suddenly discovered she had cooties.

"Thanks." He was being kind, so why were her feelings suddenly hurting nearly as badly as her body?

"I'll get you some clean towels," he said, leaving
the bathroom.

He soon returned with several fluffy towels, which
he piled on the side of the tub. He turned on the water
and placed his hand under the spout to test the tempera-
ture. When he was satisfied, he lowered the stopper and
the tub began to fill. Finally he looked at her, his dark
eyes searching. Her breath caught in her lungs. But he
blinked and broke eye contact. Without saying a word,
he turned and left, closing the door behind him.

She exhaled, trying to release the tension from her
body. Although he was gone, his presence lingered in
the room. It was there in his masculine scent that floated
in the air. In his lone toothbrush in the holder. In his
lonely razor on the counter. As she looked around the
bathroom, her heart ached for him. Every inch of space
pointed out the absence of Jeanette.

Pushing to her feet, she forced all thoughts of him
from her mind and undressed. The tub was just about
filled, so she shut off the water. She dipped in a toe,
then gradually sank into the tub. With a heartfelt sigh,
she turned on the jets and leaned back. The pulsing

water began to work its magic and the worst of the aches began fading away.

The water began to cool, and she reluctantly got out. She dried off and wrapped herself in the towel, then gathered her dirty clothes. She opened the door and stepped into Jericho's bedroom and looked around. The navy comforter matched the curtains hanging in front of the French doors and the window. The only pillows were the one where he placed his head each night and the one beside it. A navy-and-tan rug covered the hardwood floor beside the bed. Matching lamps were the only items on the bedside tables. The dresser was also free of clutter. Clearly Jericho subscribed to the minimalist school of decorating. Or he'd removed every item that reminded him of Jeanette.

Realizing she was snooping, Camille opened the door and peered into the hall. With only a towel covering her nakedness, she didn't want Jericho to think she was trying to seduce him. She cringed as she remembered that day years ago. Had she really been stupid enough to think he would betray Jeanette? Of course, she hadn't really believed he'd been in love with Jeanette. That's why she'd behaved so foolishly.

Thankfully he wasn't anywhere in sight, so she stepped into the hall and crept to her room. Pulling on a T-shirt and panties, she climbed into the bed. She listened to the sounds of the night until sleep claimed her.

What had gotten into him?

Jericho stared at the stars in the cloudless sky as if they held the answer. He certainly didn't. He'd racked his brain until his head ached and still he couldn't figure out why he suddenly found Camille so intriguing. So damn sexy. Nor did he know why his body responded immediately at just the thought of her.

He leaned against the corral fence and heaved out a breath. The wind blew, but it did little to cool his overheated skin. Nor did it remove the pictures of Camille naked in warm water that kept popping into his imagination. It had felt so good to hold her, he'd hated to let her go. Her soft curves filled his arms so perfectly he had wanted to place her in his bed and make love to her until she forgot her pain.

Frustrated, he pushed away from the fence and began walking across the ranch. An owl hooted in the distance and a horse snorted in the barn. The noises did nothing to silence the voices in his mind.

His life was taking yet another turn, and once more he was powerless to stop it. He'd gone from carefree bachelor, to happy husband, to heartbroken widower in the space of five years. He'd lived with unbearable pain for the longest time. Then he'd become numb. He thought he was dead inside. But he was wrong. The numbness was wearing off and the pain had diminished. In their place was a growing desire for Camille. He wasn't yet ready to embrace a new life, but his old life was slipping away despite how tightly he held on.

He wasn't ready to let go of Jeanette. He couldn't. She'd owned his heart from the moment he saw her. He could have sworn he'd buried his heart with her, yet it had somehow managed to unearth itself and find its way back into his chest. The beats might have been irregular and not quite steady, but his heart was finding a way to care again.

Whistling for Shadow, who was running around a scarred tree, Jericho climbed the stairs, admitting tonight wouldn't be the night he figured out a way to handle his attraction to Camille. He bolted the door, something he'd rarely done in the past. Although he knew it was next to impossible for someone to track Camille to his ranch, he took his job to protect her seriously.

He took a quick shower, then hopped into bed. It hadn't felt so big and so empty in months. He'd long since passed the stage where he would reach his arm across the cool mattress hoping to feel his wife one more time. He now realized he would encounter nothing more than cold sheets and an even colder pillow.

He was drifting off to sleep when he heard cries coming from the guest room. Wide awake, he jumped up. Because Camille was just down the hall, he'd begun sleeping in boxers instead of in the nude. Not wanting to barge into her room wearing just his underwear, he hopped into his discarded jeans and fastened them as he raced through the hall. He pushed open her door without knocking.

She sat on the bed, gripping her right calf. Tears streamed down her face and dropped onto her T-shirt.

Without giving thought to his actions, he crossed the room and sat beside her on the bed. She looked up, her teeth catching her bottom lip as if to hold back another moan. "Sorry. I didn't mean to wake you."

"I wasn't sleeping." The blanket had fallen off the side of the bed, leaving her luscious body uncovered. Her T-shirt was twisted around her waist, revealing her tempting thighs. His eyes swept over her shapely legs before he forced them to her face. "Charley horse?"

She nodded. "Plural. It's like my lower body is one big painful cramp." She gasped, then writhed in pain.

He cursed under his breath.

"That about sums it up."

"I should have offered you a painkiller earlier." But by then he'd reached his limits of control. She'd felt like heaven with her back pressed against his chest, her legs between his, her round bottom nestled against him. Her feminine scent had teased his nostrils, arousing him. He'd been afraid he might act on his desires, so he'd left her alone in his bathroom and headed for the hills.

"I should have asked." She moaned and began massaging her other leg.

It was too late to worry about it now. "I'll be right back."

He grabbed a bottle of painkillers from the bathroom, then hurried to the kitchen, where he filled a glass with water. Thinking she could use more hydration, he filled a large pitcher and brought that, too.

"Take these," he said, handing her two pills and the glass of water.

"Thanks." She swallowed the tablets along with half the water and placed the glass on the bedside table.

"Finish it. Water will help fight the cramps. I've brought more for later." He waited until she had downed every drop, then took the glass. "Lie down on your stomach."

She didn't question him, but immediately followed his instructions. That alone showed him just how much she was suffering. Camille didn't like being bossed around and she had a comment about everything. She adjusted the T-shirt so that it covered her round bottom and the tops of her thighs, then lay still. Bathed in the moonlight streaming through the open window, she was every man's dream. Or at least his. At this moment she was also his greatest torment.

Telling himself to focus on relieving her pain and not her soft, smooth legs, he began to massage the calf she had been gripping.

Her gasp filled the silent room, and he realized she must be as shocked as he felt. Before today they had done very little touching. Now his hands were going to be all over her body. Beads of sweat broke out on his brow.

"I think a massage will help. That is, if it's okay with you." His voice was a raspy whisper; he didn't sound at all like himself.

"It's fine."

"I have some liniment that will work these cramps out." Starting with her right calf, he began to squeeze the tense muscles beneath the silky-soft skin. Kneading first with his thumb and adding pressure with his palm and the rest of his hand, he increased the pressure and began moving close to her knee and then back toward her ankle. Her breathy sigh of pleasure let him know he was doing something right. Of course, the feel of her skin beneath his hands was driving him crazy. It took every ounce of his hard-earned discipline to keep his mind squarely where it belonged and not on the pleasure that could result from such intimate contact.

He wiped the back of his hand across his damp forehead. How long could he endure this sweet torture? Her skin was smoother than he'd imagined. Forcing himself to keep from turning the touch into something sexual, he began to work the knots out of the muscles in her left calf. This had to be the worst kind of punishment known to man. With each of her pleasured sighs, his jeans became tighter until they were downright uncomfortable. Thank goodness she was lying on her stomach with her face away from him or she would see just how aroused he was becoming.

Telling himself to think of the feeding schedule, he slid his hands over the back of her knees and to her thighs. He stilled and waited for her reaction. When she didn't protest, he continued to rub her skin, focusing attention on places where he felt knots.

When he'd done all he could to relieve her pain, at least to the parts of her body he dared to touch, he stood, careful to avoid the ribbon of moonlight shining through the slightly open curtains. "How's that? Better?" His voice sounded ragged even to his own ears.

"Much." She slowly turned over and smiled softly. "Your hands are magic. I don't think I've ever felt anything as good in my life."

"Glad I could help." He hurried to the door and away from the temptation to show her something that could feel even better. "Be sure to drink more water. Good night."

He closed the door behind him even as she called good-night to him. Leaning against the wall, he let out a heavy sigh. He'd escaped with his life. But barely. He was in deep trouble here.

Camille heard her good-night echo in the empty place where Jericho had stood only moments ago. Her legs still tingled from the warmth of his hands, and as he'd promised, the cramps were all but gone.

She'd been in such agony she'd wondered if she would be able to sleep at all that night. Within a few minutes he'd worked away the worst of her charley horses and the pain had become manageable. She could have told him he could stop, but she hadn't. The feel of his masterful hands caressing her body was so good she hadn't wanted it to end. She'd become more aroused than she'd ever been. Had he been able to tell when her moans changed from pain to pleasure? Probably. He'd been married for years and would recognize the sounds of an aroused woman. Perhaps he'd left so abruptly because he didn't share her feelings and didn't want to embarrass her.

Humiliation made her cheeks flame. She was lusting after him, and he couldn't wait to get away from her. She knew he didn't desire her. He was still in love with Jeanette. He'd reminded her of that only days ago.

She needed to keep her growing attraction to herself. If she didn't, embarrassment would be the least of her concerns. He might feel so uneasy around her he'd ask her to leave. She had no place else to go, so she needed to stay on his good side.

She liked spending time with him and thought he felt the same. But maybe he didn't. Perhaps he resented her intruding on his private time. Although the thought made her sad, she knew what had to be done. Starting tomorrow she would keep her distance and give him back his privacy.

Chapter Ten

Jericho stood at the top of the stairs and listened. No sound came from Camille's room. The sun had only just broken over the horizon, so she was probably asleep. His stomach clenched as he remembered how much pain she'd been in last night. No doubt she had a hard time sleeping, so it would be wrong to disturb her. He'd tossed and turned himself, but for an entirely different reason.

He'd lain in bed awake for hours, remembering the way her soft skin had felt. Given the way he'd gotten turned on, he should be grateful for the time alone. He needed to get his head together. No matter how many times he tried to convince himself that he wasn't being disloyal to Jeanette, he still felt guilty about being attracted to Camille. Heck, sometimes he felt guilty for being alive when Jeanette and their baby weren't. He knew Jeanette would want him to move on with his life, but that didn't seem fair. But fair or not, she was gone. And he was still attracted to Camille.

He descended the stairs and switched on the coffeemaker, then let Shadow out and filled the dog's food and water bowls. When Shadow returned, he wandered from room to room as if searching for Camille, whining when he failed to find her. Apparently Jericho wasn't the only one who'd gotten used to Camille. She was making a place in their lives whether Jericho wanted her to or not.

Wishing he could whine out his discontent as easily as his canine friend, Jericho filled his mug and headed to the barn. He cleaned the stalls quickly, but the task wasn't as enjoyable as it had been yesterday. He missed Camille's soft singing and her generally happy demeanor. Several times he stopped working and listened, imagining he'd heard her footsteps only to be greeted by silence.

A glance at his watch confirmed that it was almost nine o'clock. She should be awake by now. Then why hadn't she come to find him? Shouldn't she at least let him know she was feeling better? *Something.*

Was she still sore? Did she hurt too badly to get out of bed? He knew Camille needed to keep busy so she wouldn't focus on her fears. Or was her absence due to something else entirely? Had she realized he had become aroused last night? He'd done his best to disguise his reaction, but some things a man just couldn't hide. Perhaps she felt uncomfortable around him now.

He recalled his angry words to her the night she first arrived. He'd thrown the past in her face, taunting her about her attempted seduction. Even back then he'd known what she was really trying to do. It had pissed him off to no end to know she'd thought so little of him that she'd do anything to keep him from marrying Jeanette, including trapping him in a compromising position.

Before she'd shown up on his doorstep, he hadn't given Camille or her opinion of him a thought. Now, though, her opinion mattered. He wouldn't play the game of asking himself why. He knew why. For the first time in a long time he was interested in a woman. Despite everything she'd done in the past, he liked her and wanted her to feel comfortable with him. To feel at home on the ranch. Maybe he'd blown it last night, but he intended to make up for that. Starting now.

He finished cleaning the stalls and then walked to the pasture to check on the horses. Certain that all was well, he headed for the house, determined to get things with Camille back on track.

The kitchen was just as he'd left it. The level of coffee in the pot was the same, and the mug he'd set out for her hadn't been touched. Images of Jeanette lying on their bedroom floor that horrible day flashed through his mind. Although he knew he was being irrational, worry surged through him, leaving a burning trail of fear. Jericho called himself every name in the book as he ran through the kitchen. He was nearing the stairs when he heard a sound coming from the den. It was a cross between a sob and a groan.

Breathing hard, he spun around and headed in that direction. He pushed open the partially closed door. It banged loudly against the wall, causing a picture to fall from its hook. Camille, who had been sitting at his desk, jumped and screamed.

"What's wrong?" she asked. Her face had paled, and she was shaking.

"I was about to ask you the same thing. You didn't come down for breakfast and now you're crying." His heart was still pounding in his chest, but now that he could see that Camille was physically unharmed it was starting to slow.

She wiped a hand across her wet cheek. He noticed that her eyes were filled with pain seconds before she blinked and removed all expression from her face. "Nothing."

"Oh, come on. Don't give me that. We're friends. You can tell me what's wrong."

She stared at him for a long moment before bursting into tears. "Are we friends, Jericho? Or are we making the best of a horrid situation? I know you didn't want me here, but I made you feel guilty so you would let me stay. Then I intruded on your life. You must be getting sick of me. Be honest. Are you counting the minutes until you will be rid of me?"

Her shoulders were shaking, and she was sobbing uncontrollably. Pain pierced his heart at her sorrow. He crossed the room, wrapped his arm around her waist and led her to the leather couch against the far wall. "Let's sit down."

Nodding, she let him help her to sit. He waited until the worst had passed. She huffed out a breath, then wiped her eyes with the hem of her shirt. Finally she met his eyes.

"What happened?" he asked quietly. "We had a lot of fun yesterday. At least I did. Did you?"

She nodded.

"What changed between then and now?"

Her chest lifted as she inhaled deeply then blew out a gusty breath. Embarrassment flickered across her face, yet she held his gaze. "I had a nightmare and I panicked."

"About…"

"About the people who are after me. People I once thought of as friendly coworkers hired someone to kill me. That's kind of scary."

"Not kind of. It is scary. And I know that no matter how many times I reassure you that you're safe here, your fear won't totally vanish. Which is why I think we need to bring Trent into the loop." She shook her head. "I'm not going to push you. I know where you stand. But the next time you're feeling especially nervous, come to me. I promise I won't turn you away."

Her spine lost some of its rigidness as the tension left her body. For a brief moment he thought she might lean her head against his chest, but she didn't, leaving him disappointed. She spoke so softly he could barely hear her. "I was worried that you were getting tired of me. I know my presence here has changed your life."

That it had. But his life had needed changing. He hadn't been raised to mope and have pity parties. All his life he'd been told that life was a gift, and the best way to show his appreciation was to live it to the fullest. He hadn't come close this past year. True, he'd needed time to mourn Jeanette's loss, but he had gone past mourning to wallowing. He hadn't felt grateful. Hadn't wanted his life. But he was alive even if Jeanette was not. She would be ashamed if she could see the way he'd been behaving. He certainly hadn't honored her memory or the life they'd shared.

"I admit I wasn't glad to see you when you arrived,

but you're what I needed. I was sleepwalking through life, and you've helped me to wake up. You're welcome to stay as long as you need."

She smiled and his heart jumped in response. "Thanks." Her smile faded. "There's more. I just checked my email. There was one I hadn't read. It was sent by Agent Delgado before his accident, the day I overheard my boss plotting to kill me. There's been a setback. They thought they knew the identity of the traitor inside the agency. Now it looks like there is more than one, although he doesn't know who it is. How can that be possible? Are there really that many corrupt people in our government?"

"Did he say anything else to indicate you were in more danger than before?"

"No. He hasn't written to me since then. I just thought I would be able to go home by now."

Jericho's heart sank at her words. Go home? He wasn't ready for her to leave. He liked having her around and couldn't imagine not seeing her beautiful face every day. But he realized that just because his feelings had changed didn't mean hers had. She'd come to the Double J only out of desperation. To her, the ranch must seem like prison.

"You're ready to get out of this stinking fresh air?" he joked, trying to cover his disappointment.

She frowned, looking absolutely miserable. "My life is going on without me."

"That's an odd way to put things. You're living your life even if you're not in New York."

"Maybe. And I was thinking about Rodney. We used to get together for lunch when I lived in Chicago. When I moved to New York we kept in touch by phone. We talk once or twice a week. He's back from the Bahamas by now. What if he tries to reach me?"

"Can you send him an email letting him know you're safe?"

"And then what? He wouldn't be satisfied by that. He'd insist on seeing me. And if someone is following him, that would put all of us in danger. I would never forgive myself if something happened to him because of me."

"Then you're doing the right thing by not contacting him. Once this is over he'll be angry, but he'll be so glad you're safe he'll forgive you."

"You're right. Thanks for listening to me." She gave a little laugh that was a pale imitation of her real one. "I guess I went a little crazy there for a minute. I'm okay now."

"You know what you need? A change of scenery."

"What do you suggest?"

"A trip to the beach."

"A beach? Around here?"

"Yes. There's a beach in Sweet Briar. We didn't pass it because we stayed downtown. It's just what the doctor ordered." She needed to get off the Double J before she went stir-crazy.

"I'm not sure about that. What if someone sees me?"

"At the beach? If I was tracking you down, the last place I would think to look would be a beach in North Carolina."

"True, but I don't have a suit."

The thought of Camille in a bikini conjured up images of them getting soaked in the tide before he removed the scraps of fabric. Not something he should be thinking of now. "We won't swim. We can take some sandwiches and have a picnic. How does that sound?"

A smile lit her face. "It sounds great."

"This place is fabulous," Camille said as she spread a blanket on the sand and sat down. Shadow immediately dropped beside her and placed his head on her lap. Camille rubbed the dog's soft fur.

Jericho set the wicker picnic basket onto the blanket, then squatted beside her. "What do you want to do first?"

Camille leaned back, reclining on her elbows and soaking up the atmosphere. The sun was shining in the clear blue sky, providing just the right amount of heat. A gentle breeze fluffed her hair, blowing strands into her eyes. She brushed it behind her ear. She didn't have a headband, so she imagined she'd be doing that quite often today. Not that she minded. Nothing could ruin this day.

She slipped off her sandals, then stuck her toes into the warm sand until her feet were entirely covered. She wiggled her toes and the space between them was filled with sand.

"Ah, so we're burying ourselves in sand up to our necks. Cool. It's a lot easier if you lie down."

"I'm simply letting my feet relax, not planning on burying myself." She glanced at the ocean. The waves were large, but they didn't seem to be deterring other beachgoers. Several teen girls in itty-bitty bikinis were bobbing in the shallow water near the shore and sneaking peeks over their shoulders at teenage boys who were rough-housing in deeper water. The boys' raucous laughter filled the air, and Shadow barked as if replying.

Farther down the beach, several industrious little kids were filling blue and red plastic buckets with sand, dragging the buckets to the water's edge, and then turning them over, dumping the sand into the waves. They watched, cheering as the water slowly washed away the mounds of sand, then hurried back to begin scooping sand into the buckets again. She watched them for a bit, not quite understanding their glee, then shrugged. If it was fun to them that was all that mattered.

She dug a chewed-up tennis ball from the canvas bag filled with Shadow's treats and tossed it to Jericho. Standing, she brushed sand from her pink cotton shorts. "How about if we gather some seashells. Are there any along this stretch of beach?"

He caught the ball with one hand and threw it back. "Probably. To be honest, that's more of a female activity."

She flipped him the ball, this time a bit harder. "Got it. I'll pick them up and you can stand around looking suitably masculine."

He struck a pose and flexed his muscles. He was goofing around, but it didn't detract from his appeal. Dressed in khaki shorts and a sleeveless T-shirt, he looked sexier than any man had the right to. Desire shot through her like a bullet from a gun, with lots of potential for damage to her heart.

He tossed the ball back to her.

She caught it and put a hand on her hip. "I've never owned a dog, but I'm sure we should be throwing the ball to him and not back and forth to each other. He'll never learn how to fetch this way."

"Cute. To be honest, I don't think this dog is smart enough to learn how to fetch. Watch." He took the ball and threw it a short distance down the beach. Shadow barked and chased after it. Then he picked up the ball with his mouth, ran between Jericho and Camille and back down the beach, and dropped the ball where Jericho had thrown it. Camille laughed and Jericho just shook his head.

They walked across the sand. When they reached the ball, Camille picked it up and threw it a bit farther.

"Did you ever have a pet?" Jericho asked as they followed Shadow, who was scampering after the ball.

"No. My mother's afraid of dogs and allergic to cats."

"What about a fish? Or a turtle?"

She shook her head, remembering how at nine years old she'd begged her father to let her have a goldfish. Rodney, who was five years older than her, had offered to pay for it and help care for it. Her father had rebuffed him. "My parents worship at the altar of the almighty dollar. My father was adamant that we not have anything that would cost money unless it provided value in return. A dog could be protection, but a goldfish only swam around in circles all day."

"Don't take this the wrong way, but your dad's an idiot."

"I don't think there's a right way that can be taken." She smiled, though, because she'd often thought the same thing but had never dared to say it.

Shadow returned with the ball. Before he could make his escape, Camille snatched the ball from his teeth and rubbed him. "Good boy."

Shadow barked, wagging his tail. Camille threw the ball again, and Shadow took off after it. This time Shadow didn't return with the ball, but instead stayed where it had been thrown, chewing it happily. Camille took it from him and threw it a short distance. She called to him, and he returned with the ball in his mouth. She rubbed him until he dropped it, and rubbed him some more. They repeated the process several times. She was determined to teach this dog how to fetch before she went back to New York.

After twenty minutes or so of mostly unsuccessful attempts to teach Shadow the game, the dog plopped beside them, his tongue lolling from his mouth. Jericho rubbed the dog's head. "Tired?"

They returned to the blanket. Jericho filled a bowl with water and Shadow drank most of it. Jericho snapped a leash on the dog and then smiled at Camille. "Ready to gather some seashells?"

"Absolutely." She walked along the beach, her toes getting soaked by the little waves rolling in and leaving foam and the occasional tiny shells behind on the shore. The water tempted her and she longed to jump in, but thought better of it.

She scooped up the biggest shell and showed it to Jericho, who nodded. They walked in companionable silence while she picked up shells now and then. At first she kept only the perfect ones, tossing back the broken or cracked ones. When she realized what she was doing, she froze, her hand hovering over a shell.

Just what did that say about her? Did she think only perfect things had value? That anything with the slightest flaw was worthless? No, of course not. She picked up several cracked and broken shells and added them to her collection. A shell didn't need to be perfect in order to be worth collecting. It had its own unique beauty and value.

Jericho picked up a rock and skipped it across the

water. It touched down five times before finally sinking. He seemed content to walk in silence, but she wasn't. She wanted to know how he had become the man she was getting to know.

"Tell me about your childhood. What kind of kid were you?"

He grinned and for a moment she could picture him as a ten-year-old boy getting into all kinds of mischief. "I was your average kid."

"Somehow I doubt that. There doesn't seem to be anything average about you." The words burst out of her mouth of their own volition. When she realized how they must have sounded, her face burned with embarrassment. She wasn't flirting with him, but it could be construed that way. Given their history, she tried not to say things that sounded like a come-on. She hoped he wasn't recalling the time she'd shown up in his hotel room. She regretted that bit of insanity more with each passing day.

"Perhaps I should have said I was a typical kid."

She doubted that was true either. He was too extraordinary as a man.

"A ranch is different from the city. There's so much space and freedom. But there's also a lot of responsibility." He picked up another rock, tossed it in the air a couple of times, then bounced it off the waves. Four hops this time. "The Double J has been in our family for generations. Over the years parcels were sold off. When my parents took over they only had fifteen acres."

"*Only* fifteen acres? That's a lot."

"To a city girl, sure. For a rancher, not so much. They managed to buy back more. The land mattered to them, sure, but not for the sake of owning more. My father wanted us to grow up the way he had, on Jones land. The land is our birthright."

"That's nice, but it's on the surface. What lessons did your parents want you to learn? What did they value?"

He answered without hesitation. "Life. They believed life was meant to be enjoyed. They didn't act foolishly, but they believed in living in the moment. They told us to pursue our dreams." He stopped walking and rubbed his chin. "I guess I've gotten away from that lately. Of course, there wasn't much to enjoy once the love of my life died."

"No," Camille agreed.

"I guess I need to get back to that way of living."

"It sounds like a nice way to live. I think I should give it a try."

"I'll help." Without another word, he scooped her into his arms and strode into the water, the waves crashing against him.

"What are you doing?" she screeched, tightening her arms around his neck. Barking, Shadow jumped into the water and began to circle Jericho's legs.

"I saw the way you kept looking at all the people swimming and playing in the water. The longing is written all over your face."

"I don't have on a suit," she protested. The water was already swirling around his waist. Clearly he didn't care about getting his clothes wet.

"A suit is not required, City Girl. All you have to do is enjoy the moment."

He swung her over the water, and she squealed. He pulled her back against his muscled chest, and she inhaled deeply, getting a lungful of exhilarating male scent. "Do you know how to swim?" he asked.

She could lie and say she didn't and he would no doubt carry her back to the shore. But she was having so much fun. She nodded.

"Okay, then." He swung her out and back in again; the anticipation was part of the pleasure. Finally he let her go. She thrust her arms out as she sailed through the air before landing with a mighty splash in the warm water.

Laughing, she pushed to her feet, brushing her hair back from her face. Game on. She cupped her hands, filled them with water and tossed it at Jericho. Before he could respond, she started splashing him furiously. He reached for her, and she ducked under his arm, stepping around him. Giggling, she pushed against his back as hard as she could, sending him crashing into the water.

He sputtered and laughed, rising out of the water like Poseidon, only sexier. The gleam in his eyes should have made her wary, but it didn't. If anything it emboldened her. Thrilled her.

They splashed around a few more minutes, each dunking the other twice. Shadow barked and circled them as if trying to figure out what was wrong with his humans.

"I give," she said, soaked to the bones and starving. "You win. You're the king of the water fight."

"Finally. I'm glad you acknowledged my greatness." He grabbed her by the waist, then hoisted her onto his shoulders.

"Put me down. You'll hurt yourself. I'm way too heavy."

"You're fine. Of course, if you don't stop wiggling you'll fall."

She smiled and decided to enjoy the moment. She didn't want to fall off his shoulders. Too bad she was already falling for him.

Chapter Eleven

Camille grabbed the bottom of her T-shirt, wringing as much water from the fabric as she could. Still, it clung to her torso, giving him a view of her spectacular body. She had firm breasts that his hands ached to touch. But he wouldn't. She wasn't his to touch. He wasn't ready for any kind of relationship, and he didn't believe in having sex just for the sake of having sex. He believed she felt the same way. It would be wrong to lead her on if there was no future for them.

He was tied to his ranch and couldn't imagine living anywhere else. Camille was a city girl through and through. Although she seemed to be enjoying her time here, all things considered, he didn't delude himself into believing she would consider making her life here once her troubles were over. Hadn't she just said that her life was going on without her? If that didn't mean she was tied to New York, nothing did. She was making the best of the situation even as she was counting the seconds until she could kick the North Carolina dirt from her shoes.

He didn't blame her. In New York, entertainment was within walking distance. The Double J was nearly an hour's drive from everything. Restaurants, movies. Hospitals. Especially hospitals. If he had lived closer to Willow Creek and Jeanette's obstetricians, Jeanette might not have died. The doctors had all said differently, but what did they know?

He shook his head. Why was he even thinking about this? Once the people after Camille were caught, she would go back to New York, where she belonged. And he'd be alone again.

Camille caught his eyes and smiled at him. She was more carefree than he'd ever seen, and every thought vanished from his mind. Except for one. She was truly beautiful. When she stopped being so serious and focused on getting ahead, she was absolutely stunning.

She stepped closer, her hips swaying seductively. "That was so much fun. Thanks."

"No need for thanks. I enjoyed it, too." He pulled his wet T-shirt over his head and twisted it, keeping his hands busy so they wouldn't encircle her tiny waist.

"Now I'm starving."

So was he. But not for turkey and Swiss on rye. "Me, too."

She grabbed his hand. Her touch warmed his heart and heated his blood.

Shadow raced ahead of them to the blanket, turning in circles before he dropped onto the sand. He raised his head and whined when they opened the basket, sniffing the air. "Oh, no you don't," Jericho said when the dog eyed their lunch. "You have food of your own."

He dug out a few treats and tossed them to Shadow. After wiping his hands on his shorts, Jericho took the paper plate Camille handed him.

"He's such a sweet dog, if a little..." Her voice trailed off.

"Slow? Dimwitted?"

"I was going to say *challenged*. I just don't understand why he doesn't know how to fetch."

Jericho shrugged. "You got me there."

"How old is he?"

"Almost two years. He was a birthday gift from Jeanette. A week later we found out she was pregnant. She loved the idea of our baby having a dog. We both did."

Camille nodded, a faraway expression on her face. She almost seemed sad. He'd give anything to know just what was going on inside her head. A woman's mind was a mystery to him. It was as if women deliberately confused men to keep them off balance. A man's mind was direct. Straight. A woman's mind was like a Rube Goldberg gadget with all kinds of random twists and turns.

"Jericho? I thought that was you."

He turned and stood at the sound of Joni Danielson's voice. Sister to one of his best friends, and a friend in her own right, Joni was crossing the sand in an unhurried way. When she reached him, she kissed his cheek.

"I'm so glad I saw you. You've saved me a trip out to the ranch. I have dinner for you at the house."

He shook his head. "I thought Brandon would be too busy to make me food."

"Not a chance. It will take more than owning a restaurant and a new fiancée to get my brother to forget his friends." Joni stepped around him and approached Camille, who was now standing. "And speaking of friends, I'm Joni."

"I'm Camille." There was an unreadable expression on her face.

"It's nice to meet you. I heard that Jericho had been seen shopping and at the diner with a woman, but I couldn't believe it. Because there's absolutely no way Jericho would come to town and not stop by and say hello to me." She flashed him a fake frown.

"It was just a short trip," he explained. "We really weren't in town very long."

"You're forgiven." Joni's smile included Camille. "How long will you be visiting?"

Camille shifted from one foot to the other. She was keeping her presence here a secret. Not that anyone in Sweet Briar would be connected to the criminals in New York, especially Joni. "It's open-ended."

"Good. Well, if you get tired of only horses and Jericho for company, give me a call. Jericho knows my number. I can get a few friends together and we can have a girls' night out."

Camille's eyes widened in obvious surprise. Clearly she wasn't used to people being so friendly. But then no one was as friendly as Joni, the Sweet Briar sweetheart.

"The other reason I planned to stop by is to see if I can bring a few kids to ride this Saturday. They're having a hard time right now, and I think a visit to the ranch is just what the doctor ordered."

Jericho was shaking his head before Joni finished speaking. No way. In the past he'd opened his ranch to kids Joni felt would benefit from a carefree day in the country. They were a hoot and he'd enjoyed the visits as much as they had. But that was then. He hadn't hosted anyone from the youth center since Jeanette's death. "No. Now isn't a good time."

"I wouldn't ask if it wasn't really important." Joni looked from him to Camille as if she'd have a better chance pleading her case to another woman.

"I don't know what you're talking about," Camille said.

"I run the youth center in town. For the most part the kids have great home lives and just come for fun activities and to hang out with friends."

"But there's something different with the ones you want to bring to the ranch," Camille guessed. He gave her credit for being astute.

"Yes. Their mother is very ill and possibly dying. Their father's not in the picture. Their uncle came to town a week or so ago and he's trying to help, but as you can imagine he has his hands full trying to take care of his sister-in-law. The children need a break. It's got to be tough seeing your only parent so sick. Not to mention frightening. A visit to the ranch would be a break from the situation at home."

Camille turned to Jericho, her eyes full of compassion. He felt himself weakening. "Are you opposed to them coming to the ranch? Do you think it's dangerous or that they'll cause trouble?"

"No." But having children around reminded him of the child he lost. Not that he would tell her that. She'd turn that sympathy she felt for the kids in his direction. He didn't need her crying over him.

Camille turned and smiled at Joni. "In that case bring them by at eleven. I'll take them riding."

"You?" Jericho asked, disbelieving. She'd barely overcome her fear of horses. "And who is going to teach you?"

"I'll teach myself if I have to. And don't worry, we'll stay out of your hair. You won't have to do a thing."

Right. Famous last words.

He could put a stop to this plan if he wanted. The Double J belonged to him, after all. Instead he said nothing.

Joni smiled and gave Camille a hug. "Thanks. You're a lifesaver. We'll be there with bells on. I'll leave you to your lunch. I need to get back to chaperoning the kids." She turned back to Jericho. "Don't forget to stop by and pick up your food."

He nodded and waited until Joni was out of hearing before spinning around to Camille. "Do you mind telling me why you did that?"

"I want to help." She rubbed her bottom lip with her thumb, and her voice faded. "I shouldn't have interfered."

She looked so crestfallen he wouldn't have been surprised if she started to cry. He hugged her. "No worries. It's only a couple of hours." How could he be annoyed with a woman who was letting her heart lead her? Her generosity might have been a surprise before, but he was coming to realize there was more to Camille Parker than he'd once believed. And he wanted to discover every facet of her.

Camille pulled open the oven door as the timer pinged. She didn't want the cookies to burn. She slid them from the cookie sheet and placed them on a plate to cool. She'd been so incredibly busy these past few days learning how to ride and planning for the arrival of Joni's kids, as she'd begun thinking of them. Jericho probably thought she'd lost her mind, but she knew helping these scared children was the right thing to do.

Hearing their story reminded her of Jeanette and how sad and afraid she'd been when her parents died. Although Camille's parents had taken her in, they weren't any more affectionate to her than they were to Camille and Rodney. They didn't know how to be. Camille and Rodney had provided Jeanette with the kindness and support she needed to heal. Their love had helped her learn to smile and open her heart again. Camille had no doubt Jeanette would approve of what she was doing.

"That looks great," Jericho said, grabbing a chocolate chip cookie and popping it into his mouth.

"Those are for the guests," Camille said, swatting his hand as he reached for a second.

Undaunted, he snagged another one and waved at the plates covering the counter. "You've made three kinds of cookies and two cakes. Plus, there are hot dogs and burgers ready to grill. You don't really expect three children to eat all that, do you?"

"I want them to have choices."

Jericho smiled. "Trust me. I've had young people here before. They come for the horses. Everything else is secondary."

Her disappointment must have shown on her face because he stepped closer and brushed a hand across her cheek, sending chills down her spine. "Don't worry. I'm sure they'll love everything you've prepared for them. I'm impressed that you're trying so hard to make sure they have a great time."

She fought off the twinge of sorrow that came with

his words. She knew he meant to compliment her. But still, it hurt to know he didn't believe she was a kind person. He'd figure it out sooner or later. "I can't take all the credit. You spent hours every day teaching me to ride. I just hope I don't mess up."

"The kids will take their cue from you. If you're stressed, they'll be stressed. Just relax and enjoy yourself and they'll do the same."

She didn't get a chance to reply because Shadow began to bark, signaling the arrival of their guests. With one last glance at the treats, she left the kitchen and stood beside Jericho, watching as Joni pulled into the driveway. Joni no sooner turned off the car than the front passenger door opened and a boy of about eleven hopped out, a broad smile illuminating his face. His jeans and gym shoes looked brand-new.

The back door opened more slowly and two little girls slid out and stood shoulder to shoulder. They looked to be about six and seven years old. Like their brother, they wore new jeans, shoes and T-shirts. Unlike him, their faces were filled with trepidation.

Camille smiled at the boy and then approached the girls, stooping so that they were face-to-face. "I'm Camille. What are your names?"

The bigger of the two girls looked up. "I'm Megan. This is my sister, Suzanne."

"It's nice to meet you both. We're going to have a lot of fun today. Is that your brother?"

"Yes. That's Nathaniel. He's eleven."

The boy in question was chattering a mile a minute to Jericho and petting Shadow. Clearly there wasn't a shy bone in his body. Jericho laughed at something the kid said. Camille's breath caught in her chest. His face was alight with rarely seen joy and his eyes sparkled with mischief. This was the real Jericho Jones. It was good to see him appear again even if she wasn't the one to draw him out.

"Hi," Joni said, walking around the car. Her eyes were trained on Camille.

Oh Lord, please don't let her have seen me staring at Jericho.

The wicked grin on the other woman's face let Camille know that prayer wouldn't be answered.

"Hi, Joni. I was just telling Megan and Suzanne how much fun we're going to have."

"I'll bet." Joni gave each girl a squeeze and nudged them forward. "They're a little shy, but they'll warm up fast."

"How long can they stay?"

"Their uncle wants them home for dinner at five. It's about an hour's drive from here, so how about three thirty? I can come back earlier if you think that's too long."

"Three thirty sounds great."

"In that case, I'll see you ladies later." Joni gently tugged each girl's braids and waved at Nathaniel. "Have a great time."

Camille and the girls waved, and then she led them to where Jericho and Nathaniel stood. She was determined to do whatever it took to make this day enjoyable. The first thing to do was introduce the children to the horses.

Although he had helped her welcome the kids, she knew Jericho didn't want any part in entertaining them. She alone was responsible for the children. Smiling her brightest, she interrupted Nathaniel, who was still talking. "Hi. I'm Camille."

"Hi. I'm Nathaniel. Thank you for inviting us to your ranch."

Deciding not to explain that she was simply a visitor herself, she replied, "You're welcome." Jericho raised an eyebrow but was mercifully silent. "Have any of you ever ridden a horse before?"

"No. But I'm sure I can do it. I've seen lots of cowboy movies," Nathaniel piped up.

"Well, then, let's get started." She looked at Jericho, who was smothering a smile. "I know you must have things to do, so I'll take the kids to the corral and get them introduced to the horses."

"I have time." He glanced at the girls, who didn't seem too excited. "From the looks of it, you're going to have a bit of a time getting the two little ones to ride. And Nathaniel is going to burst if he has to wait a second longer. How about I get him on a horse and you get the girls comfortable?"

She had been trying to figure out how to manage just that. "You sure?"

"Yep."

"Thanks."

She watched as he sauntered off, his arm on the boy's shoulder, then turned her attention back to her two young charges. "So, do you want to see the horses?"

"In a minute," Megan said, her eyes fixed on the flower garden Camille had spent hours repairing. It looked pretty spiffy, if she did say so herself.

"What about you, Suzanne?"

The other girl shrugged. "In a minute."

"Do you like the flowers?"

Megan nodded. "We used to have flowers before…"

"Before what, sweetie?"

"Before Mommy got sick."

Suzanne stepped closer to her sister. They clasped hands. "All her hair is gone. And she throws up a lot. And cries."

Camille's heart ached for these little girls. They were too young to have to endure such tragedy. Sadly, misfortune didn't take age into account.

"I'm sorry your mommy is sick. Do you think she'd like some flowers?"

Both girls nodded vigorously.

"Okay. Here's what we'll do. We'll cut some for you to take home and give to her."

"Like a surprise?" Megan asked.

"Yes."

"I like surprises," Megan replied. Her sister nodded.

"Then let's get started."

Camille and the girls spent the next half hour choosing and cutting flowers. They were particular about what they wanted and deliberated over each bloom. Afterward, the garden wouldn't look the same, but she didn't think Jericho would mind since he'd let it become overrun with weeds. Once they had enough for the biggest bouquet known to man, Camille trimmed the flowers and helped the girls arrange them in a vase she found in the back of a cabinet.

Megan clapped her hands ecstatically. "Mommy is going to love them."

"I'm sure she will. Now let's go see the horses."

The girls raced across the grass. They slowed when they reached the corral and saw Nathaniel sitting on Buttercup. He was slowly making his way around the pen, Jericho walking beside him and giving gentle instructions. As Camille got closer, Jericho's deep voice carried to her, sending crazy shivers down her spine. She shook her head, determined not to let her attraction to this man grow. He wasn't interested in her that way. His heart belonged to Jeanette, and it would behoove her to remember that.

He looked up as she and the girls approached the fence. When he smiled, her heart leaped despite the lecture she'd just given herself. He spoke to Nathaniel, then led horse and boy to the fence.

"Look, you guys. I'm riding," Nathaniel said.

"Is it fun?" Megan asked.

"Yeah."

"It looks scary to me," Suzanne added.

"That's just because Buttercup is so big," Jericho added. "Once you start riding, you'll love it."

The little girl looked up at the horse again, then slid her hand into Camille's. Camille had never considered herself the maternal type, but this little one was making her rethink that position. Of course, the child was such a sweetheart even the coldest heart would melt just from being around her.

Jericho stooped down and met Suzanne at her level. "You don't have to ride if you don't want to."

"I don't want to. I want to play with the dog."

As if he knew he was being discussed, Shadow raced over and stood in front of the little girl, his tail wagging back and forth. Although she was afraid of horses, she showed no such fear of canines. She reached out her pudgy arms and wrapped them around Shadow's neck, giving him a tight squeeze. The dog licked her face, and she giggled as she wiped her forearm across her cheek.

Megan looked longingly at the horse but didn't budge.

"Would you like to ride?" Jericho asked as he pushed to his feet.

"Yes. No."

"Would you feel better if I rode with you?"

"You mean at the same time?"

"Yes."

"On the same horse?"

"Yes."

She nodded.

Five minutes later Jericho and Megan were circling the corral on Sapphire, one of his milder horses. He held the girl's small body securely in his arms. Megan was grinning from ear to ear. "Look. I'm riding, too."

Suzanne looked at her sister, then began rubbing Shadow's belly.

"Do you want a turn on the horse if Jericho holds you?"

"No. I don't have to ride if I don't want, do I?" Her voice trembled.

"Absolutely not. You don't have to do anything you don't want to. Today is all about fun."

The next hours passed in a flurry of laughter. After about fifteen minutes, Megan decided she'd rather play fetch with Shadow, so she and her sister tossed a tennis ball to the dog, who was thrilled with the attention. Neither girl seemed to mind that the dog didn't have a grasp on the rules and that they had to chase him to get the ball back. Meanwhile, Nathaniel convinced Jericho to let him walk the horse a little bit faster, and when he reached a trot he let out a whoop of joy.

Although the boy didn't want to stop riding, Jericho

convinced him to eat a late lunch. They washed their hands, then took seats around the patio table.

"Cowboys need to eat right to stay healthy and strong," Jericho pointed out, sliding carrot sticks beside the hot dog and cookies Nathaniel had put on his plate.

"Okay." He added a couple of broccoli stalks as well, probably because Jericho had some on his plate. Clearly the boy had a serious case of hero worship.

As they ate, Nathaniel peppered Jericho with questions about ranching. Megan joined in the conversation, but little Suzanne was content to listen.

After lunch, Jericho showed Nathaniel around the stables and Camille and the girls played with Shadow.

Before Camille knew it, Joni was back for the children. Camille herded them into the bathroom where she washed the girls' faces and hands and instructed Nathaniel to do the same. Their clothes were a little worse for wear, but all things considered, they looked presentable. Most important, they'd had a great time.

Camille handed a plastic-wrapped plate piled high with slices of cake and cookies to Joni. "I might have overdone the baking. Maybe their mother and uncle will like some, as well."

"You're a sweetie."

Camille shrugged. She wasn't doing anything extraordinary.

"We forgot Mommy's flowers!" Megan yelled.

Camille retrieved them and helped secure the bouquet in the back seat between the girls, who held it in place. Jericho and Nathaniel laughed about something and then the boy got into the car, a mile-wide smile on his face.

Joni gave Camille a hug and whispered in her ear, "I

don't know where you came from, but you're just what Jericho needs. I hope you can stick around for a while."

"It's not me. It's Nathaniel and his sisters." Camille hadn't seen Jericho this happy before.

"I wouldn't be so sure. There's a gleam in his eye that's been missing for a while. I noticed it the other day. It has nothing to do with the kids and everything to do with you, Camille. You're bringing Jericho back to life."

Chapter Twelve

"Thanks."

Jericho looked at the feminine hand gently resting on his arm, then into Camille's face. "For what?"

"You know what. For spending time with the kids. It must be hard being around children when you lost your own baby before he was even born. You could have ignored Nathaniel and the girls, but you didn't. You went out of your way to make today special for them."

"It was nothing."

"Don't do that, Jericho. Don't minimize what you did. You're a good man. I've never met a man with a kinder heart. Jeanette was right to choose you."

Her words pierced his defenses, and he snatched his arm away from her fingers. "You're wrong. I was the biggest mistake Jeanette ever made. She should have stayed with your brother. If she had, she'd still be alive."

He needed to get away from here. He saddled Diablo and jumped on his mount, turning toward the open pasture and the serenity beyond. He'd left Camille standing in the barn. But he couldn't stand there one more minute looking into her glowing face and listening to her misplaced praise.

He was responsible for Jeanette's death. No matter how hard he tried, he couldn't escape the guilt. Jeanette and their child had died because of him. Being nice to some kids for a day wouldn't change that.

Without meaning to, he led Diablo to his favorite place. He slowed the horse to a walk and led him to the watering hole. After dismounting, he leaned against a tree, sliding slowly to the ground, closing his eyes against the pain that ran in never-ending circles in his mind. The *if-onlys* returned with a vengeance. If only he'd checked on her. If only they lived closer to a hospital. If only...

The sound of a horse's hooves yanked him out of his disturbing thoughts, and he scanned the area. A moment later Buttercup and her rider came into view.

Camille didn't speak as she slid from the mare's back. Holding the reins, she led Buttercup to the water, then crossed the soft grass. She sat beside him and leaned her head against his shoulder. Her sweet scent floated to his nostrils, and despite the coldness in his soul, he felt a flicker of hope that warmed him inside. He squashed it. He didn't deserve a second chance.

After sitting in silence for a while, she finally spoke. "Tell me what happened."

He rubbed his forehead. He'd never spoken about that day to anyone. Perhaps talking about it would help.

He glanced down at Camille, who was staring at him,

her eyes gentle. Nonjudgmental. She reached out a hand and covered his. Her skin was soft as velvet. But he'd learned no matter how soft she felt on the outside, she was as strong as steel on the inside. "Jeanette wasn't a morning person."

"I remember. She used to say she'd heard there was a six o'clock in the morning, but she would have to take it on faith."

He smiled. "Living on a ranch didn't change that. If anything, the quiet helped her sleep longer. Not that I minded." He'd loved watching her sleep. There was a sweetness about her that made those times sacred. "On the other hand, I get up at the crack of dawn."

Camille smiled. "I noticed."

"I always did my morning chores while she was sleeping. When I was finished we'd fix breakfast together. Once she became pregnant, she slept even more. If she wasn't awake when I finished my chores, I'd cook breakfast and bring it to her in bed.

"That day I didn't. I was distracted by how much I had to get done. A couple of the ranch hands were sick and I told them to stay away. I didn't want them spreading their germs to Jeanette." He raked a hand over his head. "I should have gone in to check on her, but we'd been out the night before and I thought she could use a little bit more sleep."

"That's reasonable and quite considerate."

"Considerate? I was so busy working that I didn't notice how much time had passed. My wife was lying there dying and I…" He swallowed hard, unable to finish the sentence.

Camille squeezed his hand. "You didn't know."

He brushed aside her words. Camille would never

fully understand how selfish his actions had been that day. "I finished with the horses and then went inside. It was pretty late, but she still wasn't awake. I left a tray with juice and toast for her and went back to work."

His vision blurred, and he closed his eyes. He didn't deserve the relief that came from crying. "I returned an hour or so later and found her on the floor beside the bedroom door. She had been trying to get to me. Who knows how long she had been lying there. I picked her up and laid her on the bed. And that's when I saw the blood on the sheets. There was so much blood." His voice cracked; the pain was just as sharp as it had been that day.

"She'd gone into premature labor and was hemorrhaging. She looked at me with pain and fear in her eyes and begged me to save our baby. She grabbed my arm and told me if the doctor had to choose, let the baby live. I couldn't promise that. She wouldn't let me go until I did. So I promised to let the woman I loved more than life die."

He leaned his head against the tree trunk. Sometimes it hurt so much he thought he would lose his mind. But there was no getting around what he'd done. He felt a soft hand on his cheek and realized tears had leaked from his eyes. The urge to lean into Camille's hand was strong, but he didn't want her pity. Now that he'd started telling the story he had to finish it. She had to hear it all so she would know just the kind of man he was.

"I had to get her to the hospital. It would take forever for an ambulance to get here, so I wrapped her in a blanket and carried her to the truck. I could feel the life slipping out of her. We had been driving for about fifteen minutes when she told me she needed to push.

Our baby was born on the side of the road. I wanted to help, but I couldn't stop driving. By the time I got to the emergency room, it was too late for Jeanette. She had bled to death. Our sweet baby was a fighter, but he died thirteen hours and forty-one minutes later. I lost them both, and it's my fault."

"How is it your fault?"

"Because I didn't take good enough care of her. I should have tried to wake her up when I took her breakfast upstairs. If she could have gotten a blood transfusion, she would be alive today."

"You had no way of knowing what was going to happen."

"I should have done something differently. Maybe moved from the ranch. I should have moved closer to the hospital. Hell, I should have moved to Charlotte."

"Did the doctors tell you to move to town?"

He sighed heavily. "No. According to them the pregnancy was progressing normally."

"If the doctors couldn't see a problem, there is no way you could have. Jeanette loved you so much. She wouldn't want you to feel guilty. She wouldn't blame you. You need to forgive yourself. It wasn't your fault."

He stood, needing to distance himself from the turbulent emotions rolling through him.

Camille stood, as well. Before he knew what she intended, she put her hands on his shoulders and brushed her lips against his. He knew she meant the kiss as comfort, but lust suddenly burned through him, blazing a path of need. Self-loathing soon followed, and he jumped back.

He couldn't risk getting involved with her. She was more of a city girl than Jeanette had ever been. There was no way she could thrive here. They were too far away from malls and theaters. Hospitals. He couldn't bear it if another woman died because of him.

Right now, he needed to get away from her before he did something crazy like kiss her the way he wanted to. "I have to go. Can you find your way back to the house?"

"Yes."

"Good." He mounted Diablo and raced away as if the hounds of hell were after him. Maybe if he rode fast enough he would be able to forget the feel of her soft lips and her sweet taste. Maybe he could forget that for the first time in a long time his life had felt right. Maybe. But he doubted it.

Camille stood frozen to the spot, watching as Jericho rode away from her until the small dust trail disappeared into the trees. Even then she couldn't find the will to move, much less get on her horse and follow Jericho back to the house.

She didn't know why she'd kissed him. Not one of her better ideas. To be honest, she hadn't given it any thought but rather had acted on impulse.

She'd meant to comfort him. For some odd reason a kiss seemed better than a pat on his arm. Wrong. Her lips were still tingling from the brief contact while he was trying to get as far away from her as he could. The way he pulled away from her, as if her lips were poison, hurt. Thank goodness he hadn't hung around and explained that it wasn't her, it was him. She didn't have it in her to withstand that type of humiliation.

Unfortunately, his reaction hadn't dulled her response to the brief kiss. Her body was humming and had come alive in a way it never had with anyone else. She definitely had to get herself under control and fast.

In no particular hurry to return to the house, Camille wandered aimlessly through the grass. Birds flew overhead, calling to each other, their song a part of nature's music. She lifted her face to the sky and let the sun warm her skin, soaking up as many rays as she could.

The beauty of the ranch, the perfection of nature, managed to soothe her injured pride. Deciding she'd stalled long enough, she mounted Buttercup and led the mare back. When they got to the stables, she took her time brushing the horse before returning to the house.

Once there, she walked through the silent rooms, finding Jericho in the living room before the unlit fireplace. He glanced up and set a framed photo on the coffee table.

Camille looked at the picture of Jeanette in a white dress and holding a bouquet of white roses. It must have been taken on her wedding day. A twinge of guilt pierced Camille's heart. She hadn't attended the ceremony. Jeanette had been a wonderful person and a great friend. She hadn't deserved that. Camille had no doubt Jeanette would have forgiven her had she asked.

It was too late for that, but she still had time to help Jericho to forgive himself. She needed to help him reach a place of joy. A place where his smiles were real and laughter came from honest emotion.

"Is there something you need?"

His polite voice nearly stopped her in her tracks, but she refused to let hurt feelings keep her from doing the right thing. Jericho had offered a place for her to hide out when she needed one. He was still providing a refuge for her. Now she was going to help him stop hiding.

"Yes. I need to talk to you."

He dragged a hand down his face. Clearly he didn't want to hear what she had to say. Was he worried that she would pounce on him again? *Nope.* Seeing him ride away as if his pants were on fire had cured her of that impulse. "I just wanted to clear the air. I don't ordinarily go around kissing unsuspecting men. I was trying to comfort you, but instead I upset you. I apologize. I know what you had with Jeanette was special and can never be duplicated."

"She was everything."

"I know."

He let out a harsh sound, somewhere between a laugh and a groan. "I can't let myself forget. I lost everything when I lost her. I couldn't survive another loss like that."

"Then what's your plan? Are you just going to live alone in this house for the rest of your life?" The idea was horrifying and infuriating.

"I can't think of a way that my decision could possibly be any of your business."

"Maybe it's not."

"Maybe?"

"It's not. But I know Jeanette would hate it. She'd want you to mourn her death and the loss of your child. But she wouldn't want you to wallow in self-pity."

He shot to his feet, fury shooting from every pore. His eyes flashed. "You've got a lot of nerve, lady. For five years you didn't speak one word to Jeanette. You changed your phone number. Returned her letters unopened. Blocked her emails. Don't you dare try to speak for her now."

Camille paused. When she spoke, her voice was quiet, in contrast to his. "You're right. I did all those horrible things and I don't deserve forgiveness. But I do know one thing. Jeanette loved you with her whole heart. She'd want you to be happy. Seeing you like this would break her heart."

When Jericho didn't reply, Camille left, closing the door on him and the impossible dream of building something together.

Chapter Thirteen

Camille looked out the window across the acres of grass. The sun was setting in a glorious burst of reds, oranges and purples. Even though she was unsettled, she did appreciate the beauty before her. Too bad it wasn't enough to fill the hole in her soul.

Although she'd known better than to allow herself to fall for Jericho, he had wormed his way inside her heart. She wouldn't have minded if she'd been able to do the same. But his heart was locked up tight. She didn't blame him. He'd been crystal clear from the beginning that his heart belonged to Jeanette. While Camille understood that he would always love Jeanette, she didn't know he'd actually meant he could *only* love Jeanette.

She had to get out of this house. There was no way she could spend another night alone with him, especially after their recent conversation. Dropping the curtain, she tapped her finger against her bottom lip. Should she take Joni up on her offer to get together? The other woman had seemed sincere when she invited her. What the heck? Camille believed she actually was safe in Sweet Briar. As Jericho pointed out, nobody would expect her to be out and about rather than cowering somewhere.

Deciding to give the other woman a call, Camille bounced down the stairs, faking a carefree attitude. Jericho was sitting in one of the rockers on the front porch, Shadow lying at his feet.

"Hey, Jericho, do you have Joni's number? I'm thinking about taking her up on her offer to get together."

"Now?"

"Sure. Why not?" It was only six thirty.

"No reason." He looked like he wanted to say something else, but he didn't. At least he wasn't still angry.

"So can I have Joni's number?" she prompted when he just sat there.

"Sure." He scrolled through the contacts on his cell phone, then handed it to her. Sitting down in the other rocker, she dialed. Joni answered immediately, but to Camille's disappointment, Joni had a date. After ending the call, Camille handed the phone back to Jericho and leaned back, setting the rocker into motion.

She blew out a long breath and closed her eyes. Now what? Could she stay in the house with Jericho, knowing what it felt like to kiss him but aware he hadn't enjoyed the experience as much as she had? What choice did she have?

"So are you and Joni going to have a girls' night out?"

She opened her eyes and glanced over at Jericho. He

was looking at her with his intense dark eyes, and her heart skipped a beat. "No. She has a date."

"I guess the quiet ranch life is getting to you."

"I like the quiet."

"Still, you're probably used to New York's nightlife. Being here must be cramping your style."

"The fact that I want to go out doesn't mean I don't like the ranch." She leaned forward. "You used to go to dinner and movies, didn't you?"

He nodded slowly, thoughtfully.

"Did that mean the solitude of the ranch was getting to you?" she asked, determined to make her point. He called her a city girl and she was, but that didn't mean she couldn't see value in other places. "Or did it mean you enjoyed other experiences, too? It doesn't have to be an all-or-nothing thing, does it?"

He rubbed his chin as if the question required deep thought. "No."

"So why can't it be the same with me?"

"I suppose it can."

She nodded, pleased that she had convinced him. "I guess I'll see if there's anything good on TV," she said, although she didn't hold out hope.

Jericho tapped the tips of his fingers together, then sighed. "You know, if you're getting cabin fever, we can do something together."

Go out with Jericho? The whole purpose was to put distance between them. "Thanks, but that's not necessary."

"Really? Aren't you the same person who not an hour ago was criticizing me for holing up in this house?"

"Yes, but…"

"No *buts*. If you expect me to rejoin the world, you should accompany me."

"That's not exactly what I had in mind."

"No? Then what?"

"I just thought you should do something fun with someone you like."

"I like you."

Oh, her heart couldn't take it. But he sounded like he meant it. Could she turn him down when he'd obviously been considering her words? Did she even want to? The idea was appealing.

"And before you ask, you'll be perfectly safe."

"I know. So where did you have in mind?"

Jericho stood and rubbed a hand over his jaw. His five o'clock shadow was making its appearance, giving him a sexy, dangerous air. "There's a restaurant in Willow Creek that also has dancing. How does that sound?"

"Sounds great. What's the dress code?"

"Nothing too fancy. A nice dress will do."

Her heart sank as she mentally reviewed her nonexistent wardrobe. "I don't have a dress. Maybe we can do something else," she said, trying to mask her disappointment. Now that the seed of dancing had been planted, anything else would be a letdown.

"No. Dinner and dancing is just what you need."

"I don't have a dress," she repeated, even though he already knew this. He was the one who had taken her shopping.

Instead of answering, he took her hand and led her into the house. Puzzled, she followed him up the stairs into his bedroom and to his closet. Now she was more than confused. She was intrigued.

"Close your eyes."

"Why?"

"Really, Camille? Just do it."

His exasperation was cute, but he was stubborn enough to not move until she followed his instructions. And he obviously wasn't going to explain. Sighing, she closed her eyes.

"No peeking."

"Of course I won't peek. I have my honor."

"Yes, I know." He sounded so serious she would give anything to see his expression.

The old closet door creaked as Jericho opened it. That was quickly followed by a rustling sound. Her curiosity was growing, and only the fact that she'd given her word kept her from opening her eyes.

"Jericho," she whined. "What are you doing?"

"One second… Okay. You can look now."

Her eyes flew open. "That's the dress from Hannah's store."

He smiled, clearly pleased with himself. "Now you have something to wear."

She reached out to take the garment, then pulled her hand back. "I can't accept this."

"Why not?"

"Because it's too much." The price of the dress was firmly etched in her mind. She wouldn't have given it a second thought if it had been her money, but this was his money.

"It's a gift. No strings attached."

"But…"

"You know you want it, Camille."

She did.

"You'll hurt my feelings if you say no."

She was about to make a flip reply when she realized he was being sincere. He would be hurt if she rejected his gift. Her heart skipped a beat. Jericho really did care about her. "Thank you."

He smiled again. "You're very welcome."

Jericho wiped the steam off the mirror and leaned closer as if his reflection could explain why he'd asked Camille out. Did she think this was a date? Was it a date? There was a spark in his eyes that had been missing for too long. The misery that had been his constant companion had taken a hike, and the knot of pain in his chest was gone. He could breathe again. Lately there was joy inside him and he woke excited to face the new day. And it all had to do with Camille.

He closed his eyes, recalling the feel of her lips on his. The kiss had been brief, but it had been enough to send fire through his body. He was attracted to her. What man wouldn't be? She was beautiful. Sexy. Desirable. And he did want to make love to her. But he wouldn't.

Because attraction wasn't love. The soft feeling growing inside him wasn't love. He wouldn't let it be. He didn't deserve to love or be loved in return. Not after what he'd let happen to Jeanette.

He opened his eyes. Camille was right. Jeanette wouldn't want him to be alone and miserable. She'd want him to be happy and open to the possibility of falling in love again. No. That would never satisfy her. She'd want him to search high and low for someone new to share his life.

But would she want that person to be Camille, who'd hurt her so deeply? The answer came to him in a heartbeat. Jeanette wouldn't mind. Knowing her, she was in heaven cheering at the prospect of him and Camille becoming a couple. She'd always hoped her husband and her chosen family would make peace.

Deciding he'd engaged in enough introspection to last the rest of the year, he brushed his hair and got dressed. Twenty minutes later he was cooling his heels waiting for Camille to appear. It wasn't long before he heard her coming down the stairs. He turned and his mouth fell open.

She looked gorgeous. The orange-and-red dress clung to her shapely form perfectly, emphasizing her tiny waist and stopping just above the knees, showcasing her world-class legs. Her skin had a healthy glow, and her eyes sparkled.

"I'm sorry if I kept you waiting."

He waved away her apology. "You're definitely worth waiting for."

"Thanks." She shifted her feet, and he noticed she'd cleaned the heels she'd been wearing when she arrived.

He reached out a hand, and she slid her softer hand into his. They walked side by side to his truck as if they'd been going out like this for years.

They chatted comfortably on the forty-five-minute drive and arrived at the restaurant in good spirits. Jericho handed his keys to the valet, then wrapped his arm around Camille's waist and led her to the entrance. He didn't seem to be able to stop touching her.

A gentle breeze blew, filling his senses with Camille's tantalizing scent. Oh, to be able to pull her close and bury his nose in her neck and just breathe her in. But that was too much too soon. He wanted to be sure of his feelings. The last thing he wanted to do was send her mixed signals. That wouldn't be fair, and she would be right to be angry with him. Hell, he was getting pissed about the mixed messages he was sending himself.

He stepped around a couple leaving the restaurant, then held the door for Camille, who smiled at him. His blood pulsed in his veins and his heartbeat went into overdrive. Who knew a simple smile could be so powerful?

"This looks like a nice place."

He returned her smile and forced himself to push aside his suddenly erotic thoughts. "It is. The food is good and the house band is incredible. You're really going to enjoy yourself."

Her smile broadened, and she leaned her head against his shoulder. "I already am."

A hostess led them to a table near a wall of windows overlooking a garden with trees draped with twinkling white lights. Camille peered through the window at the darkening night. "It looks magical out there. I wouldn't be surprised if fairies were flitting about like in a children's story."

A week ago he would have assumed she was putting down the decorators and calling their work childish. Now he knew that a little girl who believed in fairy tales lived inside the Wall Street wizard. It was contradictory and confusing, yet he found it endearing. "Perhaps fairies are out there waiting to grant the wishes of good little girls."

"Only girls? I would hope fairies were equal-opportunity helpers."

"Nope. They can only grant wishes of those who believe in them, and boys don't fit into that category."

"Are you saying boys don't believe in fairies?"

"That's exactly what I'm saying."

"How do you know?"

"I was one."

"Exactly. You were *one*. Maybe other boys believed."

"Nope. It goes against the code."

"There's a boy code?"

"Absolutely."

"With rules?"

"Yep."

She leaned in closer, and he found himself doing the same. "Like what?"

"No can do. The rules are secret. Sharing them violates the first rule."

"I won't tell a soul." She drew a cross over her heart, pulling his attention to her perfectly formed breasts. Sweat beaded on his brow, and he sucked in a breath. Heaven help him if she really turned up the heat. He forced himself to shift his gaze to her face. Her eyes twinkled with mischief. She slid a finger across her full bottom lip. "Pretty please with sugar on top."

He groaned. From the satisfied grin on her face, she knew he was a beaten man.

"If boys don't believe in fairies, what do they believe in?"

"Well, since you're trustworthy...monsters. Dragons. Things like that."

"And a prince to vanquish them?"

"No. Princes strictly rescue girls. Boys don't need the help. When they get into danger, they rescue themselves."

"You know, I think I might want to join this club."

"Sorry. It's only for boys. Besides, there are no princes coming to the rescue and then marrying the damsel."

"Princes haven't been lining up to rescue and marry me either."

* * *

Camille could have bitten her tongue off right then and there. Why did she say that? It was true, but that didn't mean she had to tell Jericho. Now he was looking at her with something suspiciously like pity.

Darn. She didn't want anyone, especially Jericho, to see her weakness. She wanted him to see the confident face she offered to the world. Too bad he wasn't following the rules and instead was trying to get a glimpse of the real Camille. The Camille who felt things deeply and dreamed of being treasured.

Fortunately, their waitress arrived to take their orders. After a brief discussion, they both decided on steak, potatoes and steamed vegetables. When the young woman left, Camille took charge of the conversation, turning it away from her and to safer topics like politics and religion. Apart from raising an eyebrow, Jericho didn't react to the abrupt change of subject.

After the waitress set their meals before them, Camille's mouth watered as she inhaled the delicious aromas. She hadn't taken a bite yet, but she knew she was going to enjoy her food immensely.

Jericho gestured toward her plate with his knife. "I had you pegged as a broiled-fish girl."

"I like fish just fine, but if I'm going to dance, I need something filling." She put a slice of the tender steak into her mouth and closed her eyes in bliss. A small moan slipped from between her lips, and her eyes flew open in embarrassment. She saw the amusement in Jericho's eyes and knew he'd heard her. To her relief he didn't comment on her faux pas, choosing instead to continue to make small talk.

They were finishing their dessert when the faint

strains of music floated through the restaurant. Jericho explained that the dance floor was in the adjoining room. A few diners lingered at their tables, but most people rose and followed the sound.

Camille tapped her feet in time to the beat. She couldn't remember the last time she'd danced, and her excitement was building. Jericho's lips lifted in a smile, and he gestured for their waitress. After paying their bill and leaving a generous tip, he stood and held out his hand.

Remembering the electricity that shot through her whenever Jericho touched her, Camille tried to brace for the reaction. It didn't work. Tingles raced through her, and her knees actually weakened. She wondered if she had the same effect on him, but after looking at his calm face decided she didn't.

Playing it cool, Camille strolled beside him to the other room. There were several small table and chair groupings around the sizable dance floor and secluded high-backed booths lining the walls. The band was playing an up-tempo tune, and she snapped her fingers. She grinned at Jericho. "Please tell me you know how to dance."

"There's only one way to find out." He pulled her onto the dance floor. Within seconds she knew he could hold his own. As one dance led to another, she grew more relaxed and carefree. For the time being, she forgot her worries and fears and allowed herself to live in the moment.

As the last song ended, the drummer beat out a thirty-second solo, which segued into a long note held by the tenor saxophone. The atmosphere shifted, becoming intimate, and the soft lights dimmed. The musicians began to play "When a Man Loves a Woman." Jericho opened his arms to her, and the others in the room vanished. Jericho was all she could see. Camille sucked in a breath. Before she could exhale completely, she was in his arms, swaying to the music. His masculine scent swirled around her, tantalizing her. She closed her eyes, willing to stay wrapped in his arms for all eternity.

Camille realized the problem wasn't what happened when a man loved a woman, but rather what happened when a woman loved a man who did not love her back.

Chapter Fourteen

Jericho tightened his arms as Camille began to move away. Although the last notes of the song had been played, he wasn't ready to let her go. Holding her in his arms and moving to the music filled him with peace he hadn't experienced in what seemed like forever. The band began playing another song, and he led her in another dance.

For the longest time he'd felt as if a piece of his soul had broken off and gone missing when he lost Jeanette. Now the pieces were coming together again. Maybe not in the same way. Never in the same way. Camille would never be Jeanette. But that was okay. His heart could love her just as much, but in a different way.

What? His mind reeled and he stumbled. Had he really just thought that he could love Camille? No way. She was not the woman for him. Not even close. They didn't have anything in common. Not only that, she was selfish and self-centered, consumed with money and status.

He huffed out a breath. That wasn't fair. Five years ago Camille might have fit that description, but that was no longer the case. She was warm and caring— look at how she'd taken to those kids, giving them love and attention like they were her own. She had a sense of humor that sparked at the oddest times. It bordered on gallows humor, but given that someone wanted to kill her, that was understandable. In fact, he admired the way she was handling her situation. Most people would break under that type of pressure. She hadn't. She had guts.

He realized she was backing away and reached for her. "Wait. Please."

There was enough light in the room to see the shadows in her eyes. He didn't blame her for being leery of him. His behavior had been totally inconsistent. How could he explain when he didn't understand himself? "One more dance?"

After a slight hesitation, Camille stepped into his open arms. *Thank goodness.* He wanted to feel her body pressed to his, and slow dancing seemed the least complicated way to accomplish that.

The band finished the song, then announced they would be taking a short break. A DJ took over the stage and began spinning up-tempo music. Jericho didn't feel the need to continue dancing, so he led her to a vacant booth. As they sat down, she smothered a yawn.

"Sleepy?"

"No." She yawned again.

He raised an eyebrow.

"Okay. Yes. I can't believe I'm already sleepy. It's barely eleven o'clock. Who falls asleep this early on a Saturday night?"

"Getting up at the crack of dawn is catching up with you."

"Maybe, but it's worth it. Seeing the sun rise over the horizon is… I don't know."

"Magical."

Her sparkling eyes met his. "Yes. That's it exactly. Something special happens in those quiet moments. It's like confirmation that the day before is truly gone, taking with it all its troubles. The new day is a blank slate filled with promise and endless possibility. I love that feeling."

"In that case, we should get going so we can get you into bed."

Her mouth fell open in shock, and then she laughed.

He didn't mean that the way it sounded, but he didn't correct himself. No doubt he'd only dig the hole deeper.

"You're right. We need to go." She stood. He took her hand, leading her through the crowd to the exit. Halfway there, she stopped, turned slightly. "I can't remember when I enjoyed myself this much. I know you would have preferred spending a quiet evening at home, so thanks."

"I didn't do it just for you. I had a great time, too." He'd spent too much time feeling sorry for himself over what had been taken from him. Along the way he'd lost sight of what he still had. He had a lot to live for. He just needed to be open to the possibilities.

Camille and Jericho walked side by side into the house. They'd been quiet on the ride, listening to the music playing on the radio. A low level of sexual tension hummed between them, and with each step it increased. She was aware of each rapid beat of her heart and the blood pulsing through her veins. Her skin felt tight and tingly.

She'd felt so good as they danced. When he'd wrapped his strong, muscular arms around her, she'd felt safe and protected, as if no harm could come to her with him around. More than that, she'd felt as if she belonged in his arms. As if her place was with him. How insane was that? Her place was in New York, not on the Double J. Besides, he still loved Jeanette. Unfortunately, knowing that didn't change the way her rebellious heart felt. Though that knowledge should have dampened her ardor like water tossed on a fire, it didn't. She was still attracted to him.

"How about a nightcap?"

A wise woman would have said no without hesitation, but his boyish smile was so appealing and hopeful she couldn't turn him down. Besides, the attraction was one-sided, so nothing could possibly happen. "Sure. I'd love one. What do you have?"

His grin turned sheepish, making him look younger and carefree. "Not much, I'm afraid. I don't really drink alcohol."

"I'll settle for a glass of lemonade or iced tea. No, I think I'd really love a mug of hot chocolate."

"At this time of year?"

"Cocoa is not just for cold and snowy winter nights. Trust me, chocolate is always a good choice."

"If you say so. I think I'll stick with lemonade."

After they'd gotten their beverages, they returned to the front porch. Camille sipped her whipped-cream-topped drink and leaned back, setting the rocking chair in motion. "It's such a peaceful night."

"That it is." Holding his glass of lemonade on his thigh, with his legs stretched before him and one ankle crossed over the other, he was the picture of relaxation.

Suddenly Camille wanted to know everything about Jericho. He'd told her some things but not nearly enough to sate her curiosity. "What was it like growing up here?"

"The best."

"What did you do for fun?"

"Lots of things. I had three good friends. We spent every free moment swimming, fishing and riding horses. My one friend Billy participated in rodeos, so we would travel around and watch him." He stared into the night as if the past was flickering on a screen only he could see.

"Are they still around?"

He shook his head, and sadness seemed to envelop him. "Billy joined the army right after high school. He was killed in Iraq about six years ago. Tony went to UCLA and he lives in California. He used to come back a couple of times a year to visit his parents, but they moved to Hilton Head three years ago. He hasn't been back since."

"And the third friend?" Camille asked when Jericho lapsed into silence.

"No clue. One night Donovan drove into town to buy a six-pack. He never came back. No one ever heard from him again."

"Wow. How long ago was this?"

Jericho rubbed his chin as if he was thinking. Camille wasn't fooled. No doubt he knew how long his friend had been missing down to the minute.

"Eight years."

"Wow."

"Yeah." He drained his glass, then set it beside his chair.

"Did anyone look for him?"

"Everyone. Anyone with a car drove the route he would have taken, stopping anywhere he might have. His parents put up fliers. Billy was home on leave and he, Tony and I drove from town to town every day. We couldn't find anyone who had seen him. It's as if he vanished from the face of the earth. The police were involved, but when there were no leads the investigation stalled. Since there were no signs of foul play, they decided he must have left voluntarily. Eventually they closed the case.

"After a while people got on with their lives. His parents still put up fliers every once in a while, but I wonder if they really believe he'll come home after all this time."

"Oh, God." Camille's heart plunged to her toes, and she buried her face in her hands.

"What's wrong?"

"I did the same thing. Listening to you, it hit me what my family must be going through. How worried they must be. They don't have a clue where I am. I went to work one day and just vanished. Just like your friend. How could I do that to them?"

Her chair jerked to a standstill. She raised her head. Jericho was kneeling in front of her, his expression serious. He gripped her hands. "You didn't do this out of spite or indifference toward the ones you left behind. You're doing what's necessary to stay safe."

"I know. But I'm worried. My parents might be a little cold, but they love me in their own way."

"Of course they do. And they'd want you to stay safe even if it means worrying them."

She inhaled and was surrounded by his scent, the remnants of his cologne. Gradually she calmed and her momentary panic subsided. "I know you're right. I just needed to be reminded that I'm making the right choice."

"You are. Now you just have to trust that things will work out. Worrying and beating yourself up won't change anything. Your job is to stay safe." He squeezed her hands gently. "And my job is to keep you safe."

Camille warmed at his words, as if the chocolate she'd just enjoyed was now floating through her veins. Overwhelmed by emotion, she couldn't speak over a whisper. "I don't know what to say."

"Then don't say anything."

He leaned closer, and their eyes met and held. His eyes appeared even darker, and the intensity burning there made her shudder. Moving slowly, he lowered his head and brushed his lips against hers. The contact was brief and tentative as if he was gauging her reaction. After a long, heated moment, he pressed his lips more firmly against hers. Her body ignited and she wrapped her arms around his neck and scooted closer to him. He angled his head, deepening the kiss and increasing her desire for him.

She became aware of him slowly ending the kiss and reluctantly opened her eyes. He leaned his forehead against hers. Their breathing was labored. "Wow."

"Yeah," he said. Standing, he wiped a shaky hand across his jaw. "We're moving pretty fast here."

She stood as well, then reached out and touched his face. Her fingertips tingled as they brushed against the short stubble on his cheek. "This is what I want. How about you?"

He was silent. She dropped her hand. Of course not. He still loved Jeanette. Camille was just a substitute, and judging from his reaction, a poor one. She turned to flee.

Jericho placed a hand on her arm, stopping her. "Wait. I want you, Camille. Never doubt that. You're a beautiful and desirable woman. It's just that…"

"Just what?" Any doubt that she was a glutton for punishment was washed away in that tense moment. She needed to hear him say the words rejecting her so she wouldn't make this mistake again. Every ounce of hope needed to be smashed to prevent her from clinging to someone who didn't want her.

"I haven't been with a woman since Jeanette. I haven't even considered it."

Her stomach twisted in agony. Maybe she didn't need to hear the words, after all. "I understand."

"Do you? Because I'm not sure I do." He heaved out a sigh and dropped his hand. "I don't know what's going on between us. To be honest I'm a little afraid of finding out."

"Because your heart isn't in it."

He turned and looked at the darkness. Finally he spoke. "I would like nothing more than to carry you up the stairs and make love to you. But it wouldn't be fair to you. Not now."

Because his heart would always belong to Jeanette.

"Thanks for being honest." She started for the door. This time he didn't stop her.

Holding the shreds of her dignity together, she made it to her room without breaking down. She didn't know why she was so upset. It wasn't as if she was in love with him. Sure she liked and admired him. So what? There had to be plenty of men she could like just as much. She just hadn't met the right one yet.

He lived on a ranch for goodness' sake. Her life was in New York. Could she really be happy here in the middle of nowhere?

Yes.

She silenced the voice brutally, but it refused to remain quiet. Yes, she could be happy here. She didn't need to make a ton of money in order to be of value. She just wasn't of value to Jericho.

Chapter Fifteen

"I'm going to be gone most of the day. I need to check some fence on the far side of the ranch. Don't worry if I'm not here in time for dinner. Okay?" Jericho spoke without looking at Camille. She'd been quiet all through breakfast, spending more time moving her food around on her plate than eating. If even one bite of egg or bacon had passed through her lips, he'd eat his boots.

She was hurt and confused. Whenever their eyes met he saw the pain she couldn't quite mask. Shame tore through him. His rational mind understood that Jeanette was gone and that it was okay to move on. But the heart that had loved her so completely hadn't said goodbye. It didn't want to say goodbye.

And yet his head was filled with Camille. Her smiles and laughter. Her fierceness. The way her body fit so perfectly with his last night. How her heady scent surrounded him, taunting him to draw her nearer. Man, he'd wanted to.

Which was why he needed to get his head and heart to reach agreement. He needed distance in order to do that.

The barn wasn't far enough away to break the pull she had over him. He could resist for a few hours, but inevitably he'd give in to her siren song and seek her out, needing to bask in her presence. He would never be able to straighten out the mess inside as long as she was close enough to scramble his thoughts. Perhaps a day on the farthest reaches of his property would provide enough space.

"Sure." Camille pushed back her chair and carried her dishes to the sink. "Have a good time."

Jericho stared at her rigid back, aware that she was deliberately keeping him from seeing her face. No doubt the tears that had been glistening in her eyes had begun to fall and were running down her cheeks. He yearned to go to her, to promise that everything would work out fine, but he knew it would be a mistake. If he took her in his arms, they would end up in the same place. So although it shredded him to leave her like this, he grabbed the sandwiches and thermos of coffee he had prepared earlier and strode out the door.

The day was bright and warm and a gentle breeze blew, carrying the scent of sweetgrass and rustling the leaves in the trees. As Jericho drove the four-wheeler across the familiar acres, he allowed his mind to wander. Images of his happy past flashed through his mind. Unlike other times he'd thought of Jeanette and all the fun they'd had together, the love they'd shared, the memories didn't hurt. They were surrounded in a warm glow that soothed him.

He finally reached his destination. Although he'd told himself he wanted to check the fences, a part of him had known he'd actually end up here. His heart pounded as he reached the small clearing Jeanette had loved. Of all the acres of green grass and sunlit valleys on the Double J, this had been her favorite. She'd called it her private heaven. And they had experienced heaven here many times during their marriage.

He turned off the vehicle and just sat there letting his eyes travel over the land he had come to associate with her. This was the first time he'd been here since her death. He hadn't been able to look at the tree where he'd carved their initials the first time he'd brought her home and where she'd spent quiet times reading one of her many romance novels. He hadn't wanted to hear the frogs croak in the pond, knowing he would never hear Jeanette joke about them being princes who'd been trapped in a wicked witch's spell and were calling out to princesses to come kiss them.

Now he forced his legs to walk across the soft grass to the willow tree. They'd often brought a blanket and sandwiches to enjoy on leisurely afternoons. They'd laughed and talked while eating and more times than not had made love. Sitting down, he leaned his head against the trunk and let the memories come. He had expected his heart to ache, but instead he felt only re-membered joy.

Although he wished he could change the past and keep Jeanette from dying, he couldn't. But he had no doubt that he'd made her happy in life. He'd been a good husband. He'd loved her with everything he had within him and had spent every minute of every day showering her with that love. That was all a man could do.

The truth, hard as it was for his heart to face, was that Jeanette was gone. He hadn't had as much time with her as he would have liked—a million years wouldn't have been enough—but the time they'd shared here had been the best of his life. Now he had a choice to make. He could mourn her loss forever or he could live again.

The answer came to him clearly and immediately. He was ready to live again. The guilt and fear that had kept his heart locked up tight were gone, leaving a small but growing hope for the future.

He wanted to love and be loved. He wanted Camille.

He took one last look around the quiet sunlit meadow, then whispered, "Goodbye, Jeanette." He knew she was somewhere smiling, happy that he'd finally put his grief behind him.

Camille tugged on the stubborn weed, yanking it from between two pink flowers, then added it to the growing pile of undesirables. For the past three hours, she'd been clearing the landscaping surrounding the pool, taking out her hurt feelings on trespassing weeds. Could anyone blame her if she used a little more force than necessary?

The sound of an engine grew louder, and she was surprised Jericho was returning so soon. It was barely noon. He'd made it clear that he wanted to increase the distance between them, physically as well as emotionally, and to return to how things had been between them before last night. Before she had all but begged him to make love to her. He'd let her down easy, but still his rejection had felt like being dropped from the top of the

Empire State Building. Her heart had splattered and she had barely managed to scrape it together.

Still kneeling, she leaned forward and stretched for a weed that was hiding beneath a yellow rosebush. She yanked on it but it didn't give. *Oh, no. Not today.* She reached forward and pulled with all of her might. Finally the weed surrendered. If only her feelings were as easy to subdue.

"Hey."

Camille jumped, backing into a rosebush and scratching her arm on a thorn. The pain was immediate, and she sucked in a breath. She'd been so busy trying not to think about Jericho that she hadn't heard him approach.

"Are you hurt?" He knelt and reached for her.

She turned away from him, ignoring the flash of pain in his eyes. He didn't get to reject her, then act like he cared. "No. It just stings a little. I would have worn a long-sleeved shirt, but I don't have one." Borrowing one of his was too personal, especially given the way he'd pushed her away last night.

Jericho shifted around so he could better see the jagged cut. He took her hand and gently turned her arm, then brushed a finger across the bloody streak. A couple of bright red drops dripped onto the ground. His touch set off tingles, and the burning pain of the cut vanished. "We need to take care of this so it won't get infected."

"I can do that on my own." She tugged at her hand, but he tightened his grip, not so much that it hurt, but to make it clear he wasn't going to let go.

"I know. But I want to help."

Realizing that arguing was a waste of time, she let him lead her inside. Shadow had been nosing around in a rabbit hole that from all appearances had been empty for a long time. He lost interest in the dirt and dead grass and raced over, following them into the house. When they got to the bathroom, he nudged her knee with his nose and whined.

"Not now, Shadow," Jericho said. He edged the dog aside, then grabbed a first aid kit from the old-fashioned medicine cabinet above the sink. He scrubbed his hands for so long he might have been prepping for surgery, then grabbed a cotton ball and a small bottle of hydrogen peroxide.

"I think you're making too big a deal of this." It was just a scratch. Sure it stung a little, but it wasn't going to kill her.

"You don't want to risk an infection. Something simple can turn into a serious problem if it isn't treated carefully."

Since she knew how he'd lost Jeanette when everything had seemed all right, she made allowances for his overreaction. Despite evidence to the contrary, her heart squeezed, hoping this was a sign that he could come to care about her, too.

His hands were gentle as he washed her scratch, careful not to cause her more pain. They were a man's hands, with little nicks and cuts, calluses and scars. Yet his touch was so gentle he could have been tending a baby. She longed to feel those strong hands caressing her body. He was standing so close his heat reached out and singed her, firing up her desire. Even though she knew better, she stepped closer.

He looked into her eyes. His were filled with concern and something else she couldn't name. "This might sting a little."

"I'm tough," she joked, trying to calm her rapidly

beating heart. Once she'd loathed him. Now she couldn't remember why she'd found him so detestable.

He raised an eyebrow, leaving her wondering how to interpret his expression.

He dabbed her arm with a dampened cotton ball, and her eyes watered.

"Sorry. I'm almost finished."

"I'm fine." She blinked back the wetness.

His focus was on her arm, so she took the opportunity to steal a look at him. He was undeniably handsome with his rugged jaw, beautifully shaped nose and lips, and intelligent eyes. His shoulders were broad and strong, tapering down to a trim waist and muscular thighs, the result of the physical labor he performed on the ranch. But he could have looked like the troll who lived under the billy goat's bridge and he still would have been handsome to her. His kind heart made him beautiful. That compassionate heart allowed him to shelter someone who had been hateful to him. That heart had ignored its own pain to give three children a happy day on his ranch. How could she not have fallen for him?

"Done."

Camille snatched her wandering mind to attention. Although Jericho was finished cleaning and bandaging the scratch, he still held her arm. They were standing so close that their breath mingled when they spoke. If either of them moved the tiniest bit, their lips would meet. And yet he didn't step away. Neither did she.

The room, which was small to begin with, suddenly shrank to the size of a shoe box. She told herself to say thank you and go to a place where her heart would be safe, but she couldn't make her mouth form the words.

His eyes dropped to her lips, and her heart stuttered to a stop. *He's going to kiss me.* Her entire body vibrated with anticipation. Then he expelled a breath and stepped back.

"We need to talk."

She forced a smile to cover her disappointment. Would her stupid heart ever get the message? "You're the only man I know who actually wants to talk."

His lips quirked into a crooked smile. He tossed the used cotton balls into the trash can and put away the first aid kit. "I'll be in the living room."

Dread began to form a solid knot in her stomach, and her imagination began to take over. She didn't think he had something nice to discuss with her. He'd been too serious for that. Perhaps he was going to tell her that he couldn't force his heart to let her in. Of course, he wouldn't use those words. Men didn't talk that way. But the point would be the same. He didn't want her.

Not particularly eager to face rejection again, Camille tried to conjure up strength, but she was all tapped out. So she stalled. She washed her hands, taking time to clean the soil from beneath her nails. Next she splashed water on her face, frowning at the amount of sweat and dirt clogging her pores. Finally she removed the scrunchie holding her hair in a messy ponytail. She finger-combed her locks, then pulled her hair back into a slightly neater ponytail. There was only so much she could do without a comb. Her shirt was smudged with dirt, but there was nothing she could do about that. Jericho hadn't seemed to notice earlier, so she doubted it would make much difference now.

When she got to the living room, Jericho was peering out the window, his hands clasped behind his back.

He turned and smiled when Camille entered, then offered her a glass of lemonade.

"Thanks." She took the glass and swallowed a sip of the tangy liquid. The ice cubes jingled against each other, mimicking the jangling of her nerves. She didn't know why she was on edge. She had a good idea what he was going to say. But even so, no woman wanted to be told her attraction wasn't mutual.

"Do you want to sit outside, or have you had enough sun for the day?"

She headed for the door. "There's no such thing as getting enough sun. I love the outdoors. No matter what's going wrong in my life, there's something about the fresh air and sunshine that makes it better."

"I feel the same way," he said as they stepped onto the porch.

She bypassed the chairs in favor of the top step. Leaning back against the rail, she took another swallow of lemonade before setting the glass on the porch floor. He sat beside her, closer than she expected. Camille wiped her hands on her shorts and waited. This was his show. She looked at him and noticed he seemed at ease. This was definitely the most peaceful she'd seen him look since she'd arrived.

"I took a walk down memory lane. Or rather a drive."

"Oh." He seemed to be waiting for more of a response. She couldn't imagine what he expected her to say. She decided neutral was best. "Was it nice?"

"Yes. Unexpectedly so. I visited Jeanette's special place. I had avoided that part of the ranch since I lost her. I didn't think I could stand the pain of being there without her. But I was wrong."

"Wrong how?" Camille's stomach tightened with

anxiety as she waited for Jericho's response. Amazingly her voice sounded normal.

"There wasn't any pain. At least not the kind I was expecting. It was a bittersweet experience. It felt strange to be there without Jeanette, but I wasn't overwhelmed by sorrow. Instead I remembered the good times we had. There and in general. We had a great life."

Camille didn't know what to make of any of this. She didn't know what he expected her to say, so she nodded. Luckily that satisfied him.

"But as good as those times were, they're in the past. I can remember them, but I can't *relive* them. For the longest time I refused to face that fact. Couldn't face it. Now I have." He looked directly at her, his eyes warm. "Because of you."

"Me?" Her heart suddenly began galloping. She tried to breathe deeply but managed only a shallow breath.

He smiled and scooted closer to her. It was as if he was closing not only the physical distance but the emotional one, as well. "Yes. I spent more than a year numb and in limbo. Then you came along and helped me to stop wallowing in my self-pity."

"Me?" Why was she repeating herself? And when had she begun to speak in a squeaky-mouse voice?

"You." He took her hand in his. Despite the fact that his palm was rough, his touch was gentle. Soothing. She reminded herself not to get her hopes up. Just because Jericho had accepted that Jeanette was well and truly gone didn't mean he'd suddenly fallen in love with her.

"Camille." He grinned sheepishly and shook his head. "I didn't see you coming."

"I know. I just showed up and badgered you into letting me move in."

He chuckled. "That's not what I meant." He paused, and her stupid heart began to hope despite having been crushed by this very man only yesterday.

"What did you mean?"

"I meant that I didn't expect to have feelings for you." He shook his head and muttered, "I'm messing this up."

"No, you're doing fine." She didn't want him to stop now. Not when he was on the verge of saying something she really wanted to hear.

He raked a hand down his face, then huffed out a breath. "I care about you, Camille. Not just about your safety, but about you as a person. A woman."

"Really?" Her body began to tingle, and that stubborn hope she'd tried to pull like a weed had sprouted into a tree.

"Really." He leaned his forehead against hers. "Are you okay with that?"

Did he have to ask? "Yes."

"Good." His lips brushed against hers in the gentlest, sweetest kiss. It was as if a butterfly had landed on her mouth for the briefest moment and then flown away, stealing Camille's breath. Although the kiss hadn't lasted more than two seconds, the brevity didn't detract from its impact. Wonderful, colorful stars sparkled behind her closed eyes, and a warm sensation skipped down her spine all the way to her toes.

If one tiny kiss could have her head spinning, what would she feel when they shared true passion?

Chapter Sixteen

Camille's delicate body felt like heaven, and it was all he could do to keep his kiss light when he wanted to kiss her with the full desire that was raging inside him. Her heady scent only made the fire burn hotter. He controlled the yearning to scoop her into his arms, carry her to bed and make love to her until they were both exhausted.

She moaned softly, fitting herself more intimately to him, and sighed his name.

Unable to hold back, he intensified the kiss. She responded with equal fervor, opening her mouth beneath his. He slipped in his tongue, tasting her moist sweetness. His head spun, and he broke the contact. Standing, he held out a hand, which she took immediately.

Neither of them spoke as they walked through the house and up the stairs. When they reached his bedroom door, he hesitated. He couldn't expect Camille to feel comfortable in that room—that bed—that he'd shared with his wife. She deserved a place where there were no memories. A place of her own, to match the one she now had in his heart.

He passed his bedroom and led her to the room she'd been using. When they stepped inside, she pulled her hand from his and backed away. She folded her arms across her chest. It didn't take a rocket scientist to know he'd blown it.

He reached out a hand. She took several deep breaths while his breath was caught in his chest. Finally she took his hand, the first step in getting things back where they needed to be. "Let's sit."

She nodded and let him lead her to the bed. She sat farther away from him than he would have liked, but at least she was sitting. So maybe he hadn't totally ruined things. Still, he had to tread carefully. One mistaken word and he might not get a second chance. Third, if you counted last night, which no doubt she did. He squeezed her fingers gently. "I think I lost you somewhere between the front porch and here. Or maybe it was down the hall."

She blew out a breath.

"Talk to me, Camille. Let me know what you're feeling. Tell me what I did wrong." He kept his eyes on her face. He didn't want to miss a nuance or physical signal. This was too important. She was too important.

"I started to feel that you were thinking of Jeanette and not me just now. I felt like the second choice. Or a substitute."

He paused, thinking before he spoke, searching for the right words. "I can understand how you might get that impression." She stiffened and started to rise. He pulled her back to the bed. "But you're wrong."

"I know love doesn't die just because a person dies," she said softly.

"True, but I'm discovering a heart can love more than once. At least mine can." He waited, hoping she would respond. She didn't. Apparently she still wasn't convinced.

"I intentionally bypassed the room I'd shared with Jeanette." He cupped her face, caressing her cheek with his thumb. Her skin was delicate, and he knew now her heart was even more so. "I didn't want any shadows of the past hanging around. This is a new beginning for us. I didn't want you to wonder if I was thinking of Jeanette when I was making love to you. Being in a different bed seemed the best way to remove any doubts that might pop into your mind. Obviously I blew that big-time."

Her eyes glistened with unshed tears, and his heart nearly stopped. His mind raced as he replayed the conversation, trying to figure out what he'd said wrong. He didn't know any other words to explain his feelings. And now she was in tears. "I'm sorry, Camille. I never meant to make you cry. I'm trying to make things better, but I don't seem to be succeeding."

She laughed then, a choked, watery sound, but he'd take it over sobbing any day. A tear slid from her eye, confusing the hell out of him. Laughing and crying at the same time? Had he made things better or worse? He was almost afraid to ask. "Tell me what you need, Camille. I want to get back to where we were on the porch just now, but I don't know how. I keep saying the wrong thing. What should I do?"

She leaned her face into his palm. "Just stop talking and kiss me."

"Kiss you?" He had to be sure he'd heard that right. "That's what you need right now?"

She nodded. He was as confused as hell, but he took her in his arms, determined not to mess things up by voicing any of the questions bouncing around in his head. The scent of roses surrounded him as their lips met, igniting his desire.

He'd held back the other times he'd kissed her, wanting to be sure that he didn't rush her or misread her signals. Not this time. He angled his head and poured every feeling in his heart and soul into the kiss.

Camille sighed and pressed closer, loving the feel of Jericho's solid chest against her breasts. His warmth surrounded her, cloaking her in security she hadn't felt before. And desire. Sweet desire flowed through her, and she didn't know how or if she could contain it. She needed to get closer, so she wrapped her arms around his neck and returned his kiss with fervor. "I want more. Now."

"Me, too," Jericho murmured against her lips.

Camille smiled, too heated to be embarrassed that she'd spoken out loud. Besides, why should she feel ashamed for wanting him? Especially when he wanted her just as badly. Emboldened, she undid the top button of his shirt. When he smiled, she unfastened the second. Then the third. When she had undone the last button, she slid her hands up his torso. He sucked in a breath, then seemed to freeze before exhaling loudly.

"Might I return the favor?" he asked as he shrugged

out of the shirt, quickly freeing his wrists from the sleeves.

She grinned and pointed to her T-shirt. "No buttons."

"Maybe. But you're still wearing it."

"You have on a T-shirt, too."

He grabbed the bottom of the black fabric, pulled the shirt over his head in one smooth motion and dropped it on the floor. His chest looked even more muscular than she had imagined, and his six-pack abs were magnificent. Her mouth went dry at the sight and her pulse began to race.

"Your turn."

Smiling wickedly, she took the hem of her shirt into her hands and slowly began to lift it, swaying her hips as she bared herself an inch at a time.

"You're killing me here." His voice was an agonized whisper. Knowing she had the ability to turn him on made her feel feminine. Powerful.

"Good things come to those who wait," she teased, running the tip of her finger over his chest. Laughing, she yanked off her shirt and threw it on the floor beside his.

"Oh, Camille. You are so beautiful," he whispered reverently, caressing her shoulders and forearms, then sliding his hands to hers and joining their fingers.

"So are you," she murmured a second before his lips captured hers, sweeping her up in pleasure so unimaginably sweet it could have been a dream.

Camille felt Jericho's steady heartbeat thumping against her cheek and stifled a groan. She'd just made love with Jericho Jones. All of the boldness she'd felt only moments ago disappeared, leaving her feeling vulnerable. Suddenly shy and aware of her nakedness, she attempted to pull the sheet from beneath her so she could cover herself. Jericho was lying on it, so she gave a mighty tug.

"What are you doing?" Jericho's voice rumbled against her ear, something she found incredibly appealing despite her discomfort.

"I'm trying to get under the sheet." She gave one more yank, then let go. There was no way she could free the sheet without his help, and he didn't appear interested in moving.

"Cold? I could warm you up." He stroked his hand over her naked back, reminding her of how good she'd felt only moments ago. She'd become uncomfortable only when her mind began working overtime and doubts began to assail her, cooling her warm glow.

She could lie but didn't. "Not really. I'm just feeling exposed."

Thankfully he understood that she wasn't talking only about her body but her soul, as well. He worked the sheet free then pulled it up to her breasts and covered himself to his waist. "Better?"

"Much." She shielded her eyes with her forearm. "You must think I'm nuts."

"No." He wrapped his arm around her, and she snuggled against him. His fingers drew small circles on her shoulder. "You're feeling vulnerable. But you don't need to worry. You're safe with me."

"I know." At least the part of her that wasn't struggling with doubt knew that. That part knew her heart as well as her body was in good hands. She knew he would never deliberately hurt her, so she forced her fears away and decided to enjoy the moment rather than borrow trouble.

"Hungry?" he asked.

Her stomach growled loudly in response as if it didn't trust her to reply truthfully. "Need I say more?"

He chuckled, then kissed her lips, lingering long enough to stoke the fire in her. "I'll let you get dressed."

"I'll meet you in the kitchen."

He scooped up his clothes and was gone in seconds, closing the door behind him. She pressed her face in the pillow where his head had been and inhaled deeply, filling her senses with his masculine scent. Sitting up, she wrapped her arms around herself in a happy hug, then flung aside the sheet and grabbed her clothes, putting them on with record speed. Crazy as it was, she missed him already.

When she got to the kitchen, he was looking in the refrigerator. "What should we have?" he asked. He offered her a bottle of water, then unscrewed the top of his and took a long swallow. His Adam's apple bobbed as he drank, something that had never seemed sexy to her before. Now, though, she went all warm and squishy inside. It seemed that whatever Jericho did, no matter how mundane, suddenly turned her on.

"Sandwiches?" She didn't want to waste time they could spend in bed cooking an elaborate meal. She just needed enough food to take the edge off her hunger and provide energy for later.

"Sounds good," Jericho said, grabbing butter and sliced cheese from the refrigerator.

They put together grilled cheese sandwiches and warmed a can of tomato soup, touching each other as they worked. Each gentle caress or soft kiss calmed the stray fears that popped into Camille's mind. Jericho turned on the radio and soft music filled the air, providing the perfect soundtrack to the moment. This kitchen was more romantic than a candlelit restaurant.

Camille was focused on Jericho and still floating on a cloud when an anchor began reporting the news. Ordinarily she paid strict attention to the news in case there was any mention of the investigation at her firm, but now she was listening with only half an ear, so it took a minute for his words to penetrate her brain. When they did, she froze, giving the radio her full attention.

In what was being called the largest case of money laundering in US history, three high-ranking banking executives and two federal agents had been arrested in New York. Donald Wilcox, Henry Johnstone and Gerald Bellamy, of Wilcox, Jones, and Kirk had been taken into custody at their office only hours ago.

Her spoon clattered as it hit the rim of the bowl and landed on the floor, spattering red drops, which Shadow immediately licked clean. Shaking, she looked at Jericho, who was frozen as he, too, listened to the announcer.

"Did he just say what I think he said? I've been scouring the internet for news and checking my email four or five times a day, and nothing. Could it really be over?"

Jericho returned his half-eaten sandwich to his plate. Standing, he reached for her hand. "Let's check online again and see what they're saying on TV. We should be able to find out something."

Numb, Camille walked beside Jericho, her mind racing and stumbling over a multitude of jumbled thoughts. Could this nightmare be over? Had she managed to escape these criminals with her life intact, or was someone out there still gunning for her? And what about her job? Could she return? Did she want to? And what about Jericho? They were just beginning a relationship. Or were they? He hadn't said that he loved her. Only that he wanted her. Did they have a future? And was it a future she wanted?

She cut off the thoughts before they gave her a headache. She didn't have any answers anyway.

"Here's something," Jericho said, turning the computer screen so she could see the article.

The first few paragraphs provided the same information as the radio report, and as Camille skimmed the story, her frustration grew. She needed information about the assassins. There was no mention of them or any other arrests, but what she read in the following paragraphs stopped her heart. An FBI agent had been murdered and a second agent had been shot. And the authorities now believed that Agent Delgado's accident was linked to the investigation. He'd been severely injured and was still in a coma.

Jericho looked at her. "Wow."

"Yeah, wow." She liked the agent. He was kind and only a few years older than she was. She really hoped he pulled through. He had a lot of life left to live. Not that that seemed to matter in this world. "Let's pull up another article. Someone has to know something about whether the killers they sent after me have been caught."

They read five articles, but they contained the same information. Surely someone had to know something. "Now what? I'm in limbo. Am I safe or am I still in danger?"

"Is there someone you can reach out to? Did Agent Delgado ever mention anyone else you could contact?"

"No."

"Then I think we need to bring Trent into the loop. He might be able to get information that we can't."

Camille didn't hesitate this time. "Okay. Let's do it."

Jericho dialed and then put the phone on speaker so Camille could hear, too. She nibbled at her lip, her nerves getting the best of her until Trent answered.

"Chief Knight."

"Trent, it's Jericho. Do you have a minute?"

"Sure. What's up?"

"I've got you on speaker so Camille can hear. I'm not sure if you've been following the news about the money laundering at that New York firm and the FBI agents who have been arrested."

"I have."

"Camille works for that firm. She's the one who contacted the FBI about some discrepancies she discovered in the accounts. She's been hiding out here because she overheard her boss telling someone to kill her. We've read everything we can find, but there's no mention about the hired killers."

"Let me get this straight. Camille, you might have led killers to my town and you're just now telling me?"

Her stomach seized at the anger in his voice. She hadn't meant to put anyone else in danger.

"Hey, she was scared and didn't know who to trust," Jericho interjected.

"Maybe not, but you did. You sat in Mabel's Diner, filled with people, including my pregnant wife, and didn't say a word."

"I'm sorry," Camille said. She didn't want to be the

cause for a ruined friendship. "Don't blame Jericho. He wanted to tell you, but I asked him not to."

Trent was silent for a minute. "Okay. Tell me what you know about these people."

"Nothing. I didn't see anyone. I only heard Mr. Wilcox tell someone to kill me and make it look like an accident. I don't even know how many people he was talking to. I ran to Jericho after that. I've been hiding here ever since. The agent who I had been in contact with, Rafael Delgado, is in a coma because of a so-called accident they caused."

"Okay. Let me see what I can find out. Don't leave that ranch and don't contact anyone until you hear from me. Understood?"

"Yes. And I am sorry."

Trent hung up.

Camille hung her head and closed her eyes. She hadn't given a thought to anyone but herself. Had she drawn killers to this town and its people? She pictured the kids who had visited the ranch, Joni and the countless other people she'd encountered. And she may have put them all in danger.

"Don't cry. You didn't do anything wrong."

She leaned her head against Jericho's shoulder. She already had so much to feel guilty about with how she'd treated Jeanette. There was no way she could handle more. "I should have listened to you and let you tell Trent."

"He knows now. That's what matters."

She didn't quite believe that, but she couldn't change the past. Now all she could do was wait and hope for the best.

* * *

"I think I'll go crazy just sitting here and waiting," Camille said, crossing to the window and tapping on the pane. Hours had passed and they still hadn't heard a word from the chief. The sun had set and the moon was beginning to rise. A few stars popped out in the inky sky. The peace outside was a stark contrast to the thoughts and emotions bombarding her. She would start screaming if Trent didn't call back soon. Whom was he contacting? And would his inquiry raise suspicion?

"Let's go for a walk," Jericho said, coming up behind her. "You can pace without having to turn around."

"It's dark out there."

"I'll bring a flashlight."

"I don't want to miss Trent's call."

"He knows my cell number." He pulled her away from the window and out the door, ignoring her sputtering objections. "A little distraction is what you need."

They walked down the stairs, Shadow on their heels. He sniffed the grass, then returned, circling between their legs. Jericho took her hand and gave a comforting squeeze, which she returned. They didn't speak, both choosing to keep their own counsel. Camille would give anything to know what Jericho was thinking—no, feeling—but she didn't ask. With everything going on, she didn't trust herself to use the right words. He might be experiencing that same lack of clarity.

Things had moved quickly between them. They'd gone from enemies to friends to lovers in the blink of an eye. They hadn't had a chance to discuss where, if anywhere, they went from here. Maybe he didn't want a relationship and maybe he did. She didn't know. Right now she didn't have the brainpower to figure it out.

"Do you plan to return to your job when you go back to New York?"

"Of course," she answered, swallowing her disappointment. She'd hoped he'd at least ask her to stay. Pride was her friend. "There's no way I'm letting a bunch of criminals run me away from a job I love."

Okay, *love* might be overstating it a bit. There was a time when she had loved her job, a time when her job defined her. But that time had come and gone. Still, she couldn't just walk away from the people who depended on her. That would be irresponsible.

Jericho only grunted. She didn't quite know what to make of that. He shined the flashlight on the ground before them, moving it from side to side to illuminate their path. The possibility of tripping on a tree root or stepping into a hole required them to walk slowly. The sounds of the night soothed her, and her heart rate slowed to normal.

"Ready to go back?" Jericho asked after about twenty minutes.

"Yes."

They turned and headed back to the house in silence. When they got there, they checked the internet for updated information, but there wasn't any.

"This could take a while," Jericho cautioned.

"It's already been a while." She knew she shouldn't be snapping at him, but she couldn't help it. She paced to the window and back.

"How about something to eat?"

Jericho had coaxed her to finish her soup earlier, but there had been no hope for the grilled cheese. "I don't think I can swallow a thing. You can go ahead if you're hungry."

He shook his head, then sat on the couch. "Come here."

She smothered a sigh and joined him. He stretched out and pulled her to lie down beside him. As he wrapped his arm around her waist, she leaned her head against his shoulder and closed her eyes. The wait might still be long, but it would be easier to take lying in Jericho's arms.

The phone rang and Camille shot up, reaching for the phone at the same time as Jericho. He got to it first and answered. A second later he put it on speaker. "Go ahead. Camille is listening."

She sat as close as she could to him, gaining strength from his nearness.

"It took some doing, but I managed to talk with an agent involved in the case. They were pleased to hear you're okay and want to get your statement as soon as possible. Apparently Agent Delgado informed his superior at the FBI that he was concerned about your welfare. He was injured and then you vanished before they could make contact with you."

"What about the people who are after her?" Jericho asked. "Is Camille safe now?"

"I was getting to that. Wilcox admitted to trying to hire someone to kill you, Camille. What he didn't know was the person he was talking to was actually an undercover agent. The FBI is confident that everyone involved is in custody and that you're not in any danger. Camille, you're free to return home whenever you choose."

Jericho thanked Trent, and Camille babbled words she hoped made sense.

She sagged against the couch, her body too limp to sit up straight. "It's over. It's finally over." Then she started to laugh with abandon and relief and plain old joy. "I'm free. Jericho, I'm free. I can finally go home."

Jericho smiled, but it didn't reach his eyes. He handed her the phone. "I'll give you some privacy."

"What?" Camille shook herself and focused on Jericho.

"You can't want me listening to your conversation with your family. I know I'm not on their list of favorite people."

"Maybe before. But after the way you protected me, they're going to love you. They'll be in your debt for life." She had no doubt her family would come to love Jericho.

Just as much as she had.

Chapter Seventeen

Lost in his thoughts, Jericho sat in the dark kitchen, his legs stretched in front of him. Unable to sleep, he'd tossed for a few minutes before getting out of bed. He hadn't had a bout of insomnia since before Camille arrived. It didn't take a genius to connect his inability to sleep with her imminent departure.

When had he fallen for Camille? And how? One minute he'd absolutely detested her and couldn't stand having her around. The next he couldn't imagine living another day without her. His strong feelings had blindsided him. If he would have seen the change coming he could have fought against it before these softer emotions invaded his heart. Now he was faced with the prospect of loving and losing another woman. Hell, he'd already lost her. She was going back to New York. The only thing left was the inevitable pain.

"Can't sleep?"

The quiet voice came from behind him and he turned, wondering if he'd conjured her just by thinking about her. Dressed in one of his T-shirts that hit her midthigh and left very little to the imagination, Camille looked sweet and sexy, a contradiction that was totally her. She took a step forward on bare feet, and her now-familiar fragrance teased his nostrils, propelling him out of the chair and in her direction until they stood only inches apart. His eyes caressed her face in the way his hands ached to.

"What are you doing up at this hour?" he asked.

"I'm too restless to sleep. I can't shut off my mind, you know?"

"You must be pretty excited about going home."

She shrugged, and he hoped that was a sign that she was torn about leaving him. "It feels good not to be hunted."

"I can imagine."

"I wanted to talk to you about leaving." She gave him an uncertain smile, suddenly seeming shy. He couldn't imagine why. She had her own car and could leave whenever she wanted. He'd removed it from the shed while she'd been on the phone with her family. He'd even driven to a gas station and filled the tank for her. He hated doing that, but he wanted to be sure she was safe.

"Shoot."

Instead of answering, she sat at the table in what he had come to think of as her chair. It faced the window and had a perfect view of the Double J. At least it did in the daytime. Now the buildings were colorless shadows in the moonlight.

"I need to stay a couple more days."

"Why?" In an effort to cover his hope, his voice sounded harsh. Almost angry. She flinched, and guilt smacked him upside his head. He didn't want to turn his heartache into her pain.

"I must have sounded shaky on the phone. I tried, but I couldn't keep from crying. Rodney insisted on flying down here so he can drive back with me. The first flight he could get is for the day after tomorrow." She twisted her hands together, then placed them in her lap. "I hope that's okay. Nothing I said could convince him not to come."

Jericho tried to recall Camille's brother. He drew a blank, unable to picture the man who had been engaged to Jeanette before Jericho had swooped in and whisked her away to Las Vegas. The other man probably hated him, but Jericho admired Rodney for putting his feelings aside out of his concern for his sister. "That's fine. I didn't expect you to leave right away. You're welcome to stay as long as you want."

"Really?" Camille's eyes lit up, and despite her being off-limits now, he was filled with heated desire for her.

"Yes. You should get some rest. Morning will be here before you know it."

Standing, she reached for his hand. "You need to sleep, too. Maybe we can help each other."

He wanted to take her hand and all that she offered, but wouldn't. "That's not a good idea."

Her smile wavered, but she didn't leave. "I think it is."

"Camille," he started, then stopped when he couldn't think of an argument. He wanted her.

"No more talking." She took his hand and led him back upstairs.

Camille folded the last shirt and placed it in the shopping bag with her other belongings. First thing this morning she'd laundered the sheets and returned them to the linen closet. Despite Jericho's telling her not to bother, she'd cleaned the room, mopping and dusting until the room could pass the white-glove test. She'd even washed the windows. Looking around, she tried to keep her emotions in check. Still, when her eyes landed on the mattress, memories of the past nights spent in Jericho's arms bombarded her and her knees weakened. She hadn't held back anything, showing him with her body all the love she held in her heart. The words had nearly burst from her lips, but she'd caught them in time. This was goodbye. No good could come from letting Jericho know how she felt. After all, he hadn't asked her to stay.

She heard a car arriving outside, which meant her time on the Double J was coming to an end. Grabbing the bag, she looked around and said a final farewell to the room that had sheltered her, then headed downstairs. She'd last seen Jericho at breakfast before he'd gone to the barn to care for the horses. She ached to see him one last time. Today was an ordinary day for him, so she had let him go despite the fact that she'd longed to spend every last moment with him.

Not knowing what to expect, she hurried into the living room, where the men were eyeing each other.

"Rodney," she exclaimed, rushing to give her brother a hug.

He pulled her into his arms and lifted her into the air. He held her a long time before setting her on her feet. "I was so worried about you. I almost lost it when I heard you were missing."

"I know. I'm sorry. I just didn't know what else to do." Tears filled her eyes, and she blinked them back. "I wanted to let you know I was okay, but I was afraid I'd put everyone in danger."

He hugged her again. "I'm just glad that you're safe."

"Thanks to Jericho." She glanced over at him and smiled tentatively. He was standing there, his face expressionless.

"Are you ready to go?" Rodney asked, ignoring Jericho. Clearly he didn't want to be in this house one second more than absolutely necessary. She understood why he felt that way, but she wished there could be peace between the men. Rodney had never gotten over losing Jeanette and he resented Jericho bitterly, so she might as well be wishing for world peace.

"Before you leave, I have something I need to say." Jericho stepped in front of her brother and blocked his path. "I want to apologize for what happened with Jeanette. Not for loving her. I'll never regret that or the life we had together. But I could have handled things differently. I should have been the one to talk to you. Not Jeanette. Maybe I should have waited to marry her until you had time to…I don't know…get over her. Adjust to losing her." Jericho's voice softened. "But I loved her and couldn't wait to spend the rest of my life with her. Still, I'm sorry for causing you pain. Having lost her myself, I know what you felt. And for that I am sorry."

Camille kept her face serene even as his words broke her heart. He'd loved Jeanette so desperately he couldn't maintain his usual code of conduct because he couldn't wait to make Jeanette his wife. And yet he was letting Camille leave without a word of protest. He was just standing there with his hand outstretched to her brother, waiting to see if Rodney would return his handshake. Apparently she was already forgotten.

"I will never forgive you for Jeanette," Rodney said, his voice hard and raised with anger. He exhaled, then spoke more quietly. "But I am grateful to you for keeping Camille safe." He shook Jericho's hand briefly and walked out the door.

Camille watched her brother leave, then turned back to Jericho. Even though he was close enough for her to feel the heat radiating from his body and smell the slight scent of hay and fresh air that clung to him, he felt miles away from her. The T-shirt and jeans were such a part of him she'd never be able to see another man dressed that way without thinking of him. Not that she would need reminders.

She met his eyes. They were filled with concern.

"Are you going to be all right?" he asked, reaching out a hand and touching her cheek.

"Of course." A broken heart could still pump blood.

He frowned. Just what did he expect her to say? That she loved him and wanted him to ask her to stay? That she wished he could love her the way he'd loved Jeanette? That it was tearing her apart to leave him? She couldn't beg. Wouldn't beg. She wouldn't put either of them through that awkwardness.

"Call me when you get home?" He shoved his hands

in his pockets. "Time ran out before we had a chance to talk."

Her throat tightened, and she nodded. "I will." Her vision blurred as tears filled her eyes. She hugged him tight, knowing it would be the last time, and whispered, "Thank you for being my prince."

"Are you ready to tell me what happened between you and Jones?" Rodney had stayed in New York for a week to make sure Camille was okay. He'd even accompanied her to her interview with the FBI. His presence hadn't been necessary but was comforting nonetheless. He was returning to Chicago this afternoon, so he and Camille were having a farewell breakfast at a restaurant not far from her condo. Rodney hadn't mentioned Jericho once during the past seven days, and she thought she'd be able to avoid this conversation. Apparently not.

Camille stopped stirring her coffee and took a sip, stalling for time. She grimaced and forced it down. How much sugar had she put in there? If the several empty sugar packets scattered across the table were any indication, her teeth would rot in her head if she finished the cup.

"What do you mean?" she finally responded.

Rodney shook his head, and one corner of his mouth lifted in what for him passed as a smile. Leaning back in his chair, he crossed his arms to wait her out, a skill he'd mastered when they were kids. Unfortunately for her, he hadn't lost his touch.

He'd been the holder of her secrets for as long as she could remember, never judging her. She'd always trusted him with her innermost thoughts. But how could she tell him about her relationship with Jericho when

Jericho had caused him so much pain? What she and Jericho had shared was over, so there was no point to it.

Still, she could never lie to Rodney, so she settled on an answer that was the truth if not the whole story. "He was there when I needed him. I showed up on his doorstep and he took me in."

"I don't understand. What made you go to him? Considering everything he's done he should be the last person you would turn to for help." Unspoken was Rodney's belief that she should have come to him—her big brother—no matter the trouble she would be bringing to his front door.

"That was the point. I was hiding. He was not in my life and no one would look for me there."

"And now? If the looks I saw pass between you mean anything, he's a part of your life now. You looked pretty close."

Not sure how to answer, Camille stalled, opening another packet of sugar and pouring it into her coffee. "We spent a lot of time together. How could we not? So, sure, we became closer than we were. It would have been impossible not to."

Rodney breathed deeply through his nose. A lawyer, he always knew when he wasn't getting a straight answer. Like now. "Camille, you don't have to protect me, so don't worry about hurting my feelings. Tell me the truth. I can handle it."

To her horror her eyes filled with tears, and she squeezed them shut. She didn't want him to see her cry. A painful lump the size of a city bus materialized in her throat, and for a moment she feared she would lose the battle and bawl all over the place. She felt her brother squeeze her hand. She expelled the breath that was caught in her lungs and managed to whisper, "I fell in love with him."

Rodney was silent so long she wondered if she'd angered or hurt him. He couldn't have expected to hear that. But he was still holding her hand. That was so Rodney. He would support her no matter how badly she hurt him.

"I'm sorry," she murmured.

"Don't be."

"But you're my brother."

"Exactly. Nothing can ever change that." He sighed. "Love is a precious gift. Don't walk away from it because of me."

Now, that wasn't like her brother. She couldn't remember his ever speaking so sensitively before. Like such an evolved male. Laughter bubbled up inside her, and despite her tears she let the laughter flow. She was a mess. "I don't know how it happened. I hated him for so many years for what he did to you. Then when I needed him he was there, ready and willing to protect me. Over time I discovered he wasn't the horrible selfish person I thought he was."

"He has to have some good qualities if both you and Jeanette fell for him."

"You aren't angry with me?"

He shrugged. "Why would I be? You can't control your feelings."

"Still. I feel disloyal."

"Don't." He sipped his coffee. She met his eyes, seeing understanding and unconditional love there.

Overwhelmed by her brother's generosity, she looked away. Needing something to diffuse her emotions, she lifted her cup. Just in time she remembered her coffee was undrinkable and set it back on the saucer. She fumbled through her purse, found a tissue, blotted her tears and swiped at her nose. She gathered herself while he signaled the waitress and requested a fresh cup of coffee for her.

After taking a sip of the strong brew, she leaned against the back of her chair.

"Better?" Rodney asked.

She knew he wasn't just talking about the coffee. "Much."

"So what do you plan to do now?"

"Return to work. What else can I do?" As soon as she got over her fear of going into that building. Even thinking of stepping inside her office made her heart race and caused her to break into a cold sweat. The morning after she'd arrived in New York, she'd dressed for work, then sat on her bed for two hours before calling the office and requesting three months leave. Given the circumstances, the partners agreed, offering to keep her position open indefinitely. And they were willing to discuss a financial settlement if she chose not to return.

"That's it? You tell me you're in love with him and that you're going back to work?"

"Yep." She swallowed more coffee, then turned defiant eyes to him. "There's nothing more to do. What we had is over."

"I didn't get that feeling while I was there. You can deny it, but there's unfinished business between the two of you."

She'd thought the same thing, too. As she'd promised, she called Jericho as soon as she'd first stepped inside her apartment. He'd been cordial, but that had been it. He hadn't asked her to call again, nor had he done so himself. Seven days of silence spoke more emphatically than words of rejection ever could. She hadn't expected that from Jericho. Men had disappointed her in the past and she had survived. She would steel her heart so she wouldn't be disappointed again.

"He's not over Jeanette."

Rodney's eyes narrowed. Camille hated bringing up Jeanette because she knew how much it hurt him to think of his former fiancée. Then his lips lifted in a small smile. "It didn't look like that to me."

Camille stomped on the hope that made her heart leap. Still her voice cracked. "It didn't?"

"No. I think he's put Jeanette in the past."

"Have you?"

"Different situation. Besides, we're talking about you and Jericho. Because you're my sister, I'm going to give you some unsolicited advice and waive my hourly fee. If you love him, fight for him. Don't let that Parker pride get in the way."

Camille nodded. It wasn't pride that was stopping her. It was fear of rejection. Could her heart take hearing the words *I don't love you*?

Chapter Eighteen

The knock on the door startled Camille. The doorman hadn't announced anyone, so it had to be one of her neighbors, which was odd because they didn't know each other that well. Sure, she nodded hello to Amy Nelson when they met in the elevator. And she always smiled as Mrs. Lewis spoke to her a little too loudly. The widow could never remember to wear her hearing aid, but she never forgot to show Camille the latest pictures of her grandkids on the iPhone she had somehow mastered. But Camille didn't have the type of relationship with either of them where they would show up at her door unannounced.

The knock came again, more insistently this time.

"Coming," she called at the third knock. Reaching the door, she peered out the peephole to see who was so impatient to see her.

Jericho.

Her knees went weak and she wobbled, stumbling against the entry table and nearly upsetting a vase of flowers.

She straightened the vase, then caught a glimpse of herself in the hall mirror. She hadn't planned on going out so she hadn't bothered with makeup. She was wearing her most comfortable clothes that she absolutely never let anyone see her in. And now Jericho was standing outside her door.

"Come on, Camille. I can hear you moving around. I know you're in there."

She looked down at her cowboy boots that she now wore with everything. Naturally they would make noise on her hardwood floors.

She raised her hand to run it through her hair, then thought better of it. He'd seen her at her worst. Besides, there was nothing she could do in a couple of seconds that would improve her appearance. She swung open the door and stepped aside, allowing him to come in.

He entered and closed the door behind him. Suddenly the spacious foyer shrank to the size of the empty ice cream container sitting on her kitchen counter. Her eyes were drawn to his broad shoulders. Then she met his deep and searching gaze. She longed to be wrapped in his strong arms and held against his strong chest. Angry at herself for still wanting him, she pushed away that desire.

She turned, intending to lead him into the living room, when he placed a hand on her arm, stopping her. The warmth of his fingers made her stomach jittery, and she was suddenly unable to move.

"How have you been?" His voice was so gentle, she could almost believe he really cared.

She refused to let him know how for the first three days after she arrived home she'd run to the phone each time it rang. Or how she'd slept with it on the pillow beside her because she didn't want to risk missing his call. She still had her pride.

"I'm fine," she replied, pulling away from him and walking into the living room. "You didn't have to come all this way to ask me that. It's been two weeks, after all." Thirteen days, but she was probably the only one counting.

"That doesn't mean I didn't care. I do. I was just giving you time."

"Time to what?" she shrieked. She was furious and hurt and didn't care if she sounded irrational. She was irrational.

"Time to get over everything that happened. Time to figure out what you want to do." He raked a hand over his head, something he did when he was aggravated or unsure. She wished she knew which one it was. "Time to decompress. I didn't want to put pressure on you."

"So you just turned your back and left me floundering." She flopped onto a chair, furious with herself for letting that bit slip. The last thing she wanted was for him to know how much she'd needed him. How hurt and lost she'd felt without him. But she'd survived. He might have let her down, but her pride hadn't.

He knelt in front of her and took her hands into his. Despite her pride screaming at her to yank them away so she could appear strong, she didn't. She missed his touch. "I'm sorry, Camille. I thought I was doing the right thing."

She huffed and looked away.

"Would it help if I told you I missed you, too, and that I did some floundering of my own? That I walked into your bedroom day after day, imagining you there."

"Only if it's true. I don't need to be patronized."

"Oh, it's true all right. It's just… Everything happened so fast between us. Our feelings changed overnight, going from hate to friendship to something more intimate in such a short time. You were under a lot of stress, which can make you do things you wouldn't ordinarily do. I didn't want you to be bound to me when the pressure was off. I wanted you to be sure you wanted me even in the most mundane time."

"So this wasn't about me. It was about you."

He was silent for several long moments. "Yes," he finally said. "I guess I was protecting myself. Your life here is exciting."

"Too exciting."

"Maybe. But you couldn't wait to return. You were finally free. Free to come back. Free to leave me."

She had said that, but she hadn't meant it in the way he heard. But he didn't know that. He might have believed she was glad to shed the dust of the Double J off her feet. Given how it must have sounded to him, he'd taken a risk showing up on her doorstep unannounced. The irony of that was unmistakable.

Her anger melted. She didn't want to be at odds with him anyway. What she really wanted was to be in his arms again. Looking at him, she saw his heart in his eyes. "I didn't mean it that way. I just meant that I didn't have to be afraid anymore. I could come back if I wanted to. Not that I wanted to."

"And yet you came back."

"Yes. I had to. I couldn't just walk away from my life and leave everything up in the air."

"I know."

"And you were right," she admitted grudgingly. "I did need some time to decompress."

"How was work?"

"I haven't gone back. I just can't make myself step into that building. I know the people who wanted to harm me are gone, but that doesn't seem to make me less afraid. Just thinking of it scares me silly."

"Hey, you're okay." She didn't even know she was trembling until he pulled her to her feet, wrapped his arms around her and held her against his chest. He smelled so good. Although he didn't smell of hay and the ranch, but rather of an enticing cologne, his scent was still familiar.

"I hate being afraid."

"You don't have to be. I'm here. I'll always be here." He led her to the sofa and pulled her onto his lap.

She leaned her head against his chest, basking in his nearness and his warmth. Jericho had actually come to her. The seed of happiness that she thought had died in her began to sprout and blossom.

"Are you determined to go back to that firm?"

"I don't know."

"If you're uncomfortable, maybe you should quit and try something else."

"Like what?" She managed to keep the disappointment from her voice. She thought he was going to ask her to return to the ranch, but he was trying to help her find a new job.

"There must be other financial firms where you can work."

"Sure. New York is America's banking capital."

"I imagine working here is the ultimate goal."

"Yes." She could have left it there, kept her pride intact, but she didn't. "For some."

"Is it for you?"

"Not any longer. It's amazing how having people plotting to kill you can change your perspective."

"That's now. With time, you might feel different."

She was shaking her head before he was finished speaking. "No. I'm done."

"What are you going to do next?"

"I don't know. I'm going to think about it."

A smile began to grow on his face. "Would you consider thinking in North Carolina?"

The hope began to grow again, lighting the darkness in her heart like a sunrise. "I would."

"You would consider it or you would come back home?"

She sucked in a breath. "Home?"

"Yes, home. I need you. I miss you. Shadow misses you."

"I miss that crazy dog, too."

"You'll come back to me?"

"To you?"

"Yes. I love you, Camille. I can't imagine living my life without you in it. Marry me."

Joy blossomed in her heart and laughter bubbled out of her. "I love you, too. Yes, I'll marry you."

He kissed her then, and she returned it with the love she felt throughout her body and soul. She was happier than she'd ever imagined being. She'd gone to Jericho to save her life and had found the life she wanted to live and a love to last a lifetime.

* * * * *

If you loved this story,
don't miss the first two books in the
SWEET BRIAR SWEETHEARTS,
by Kathy Douglass

HOW TO STEAL THE LAWMAN'S HEART
THE WAITRESS'S SECRET

Available from Harlequin Special Edition.

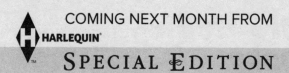
#2599 NO ORDINARY FORTUNE
The Fortunes of Texas: The Rulebreakers • by Judy Duarte
Carlo Mendoza always thought he had the market cornered on charm, until he met Schuyler Fortunado. She's a force of nature—and secretly a Fortune! And when Schuyler takes a job with Carlo at the Mendoza Winery, sparks fly!

#2600 A SOLDIER IN CONARD COUNTY
American Heroes • by Rachel Lee
After an injury places him on indefinite leave, Special Forces sergeant Gil York ends up in Conard County to escape his overbearing family. Miriam Baker, a gentle music teacher, senses Gil needs more than a place to stay and coaxes him out from behind his walls. But is he willing to face his past to make a future with Miriam?

#2601 AN ENGAGEMENT FOR TWO
Matchmaking Mamas • by Marie Ferrarella
The Matchmaking Mamas are at it again, this time for Mikki McKenna, a driven internist who has always shied away from commitment. But when Jeff Sabatino invites her to dine at his restaurant and sparks a chance at a relationship, she begins to wonder if this table for two might be worth the risk after all.

#2602 A BRIDE FOR LIAM BRAND
The Brands of Montana • by Joanna Sims
Kate King has settled into her role as rancher and mother, but with her daughter exploring her independence, she thinks she might want to give handsome Liam Brand a chance. But her ex and his daughter are both determined to cause trouble, and Kate and Liam will have to readjust their visions of the future to claim their own happily-ever-after.

#2603 THE SINGLE DAD'S FAMILY RECIPE
The McKinnels of Jewell Rock • by Rachael Johns
Single-dad chef Lachlan McKinnell is opening a restaurant at his family's whiskey distillery and struggling to find a suitable head hostess. Trying to recover from tragedy, Eliza Coleman thinks a move to Jewell Rock and a job at a brand-new restaurant could be the fresh start she's looking for. She never expected to fall for her boss, but it's beginning to look like they have all the ingredients for a perfect family!

#2604 THE MARINE'S SECRET DAUGHTER
Small-Town Sweethearts • by Carrie Nichols
When he returns to his hometown, marine Riley Cooper finds the girl he left behind living next door. But there's more between them than the heartbreak they gave each other—and five-year-old Fiona throws quite a wrench in their reunion. Will Riley choose the marines and a safe heart, or will he risk it all on the family he didn't even know he had?

Get 2 Free Books,
Plus 2 Free Gifts—
just for trying the
Reader Service!

"Sorry," she said. "I just feel so helpless. Talk away. I'll
keep my mouth shut."

"I don't want that." Then he caused her to catch her
breath by sliding down the couch until he was right beside
her. He slipped his arm around her shoulders, and despite
her surprise, it seemed the most natural thing in the world
to lean into him and finally let her head come to rest on his
shoulder.

"Holding you is nice," he said quietly. "You quiet the rat
race in my head. Does that sound awful?"

How could it? she wondered, when she'd been amazed at
the way he had caused her to melt, as if everything else went
away and she was in a warm, soft, safe space. If she could
offer him any part of that, she would, gladly.

"If that sounds like I'm using you…"

"Man, don't you ever stop? Do you ever just go with the
flow?" Turning and tilting her head a bit, she pressed a quick
kiss on his lips.

"What the…" He sounded surprised.

"You're analyzing constantly," she told him. "This isn't a mission. Let it go. Let go. Just relax and hold me, and I hope you're enjoying it as much as I am."

Because she was. That wonderful melting filled her again, leaving her soft and very, very content. Maybe even happy.

"You are?" he murmured.

"I am. More than I've ever enjoyed a hug." God, had she ever been this blunt with a man before? But this guy was so bound up behind his walls and drawbridges, she wondered if she'd need a sledgehammer to get through.

But then she remembered Al and the distance she'd sensed in him during his visits. Not exactly alone, but alone among family. These guys had been deeply changed by their training and experience. Where did they find comfort now? Real comfort?

Her thoughts were slipping away in response to a growing anticipation and anxiety. She was close, so close to him, and his strength drew her like a bee to nectar. He even smelled good, still carrying the scents from the storm outside and his earlier shower, but beneath that the aroma of male.

Everything inside her became focused on one trembling hope, that he'd take this hug further, that he'd draw her closer and begin to explore her with his hands and mouth.

Don't miss
A SOLDIER IN CONARD COUNTY by Rachel Lee,
available February 2018 wherever
Harlequin® Special Edition books and ebooks are sold.

www.Harlequin.com

Looking for more satisfying love stories
with community and family at their core?

Check out **Harlequin® Special Edition**
and **Harlequin® Western Romance** books!

New books available every month!

CONNECT WITH US AT:

Harlequin.com/Community

 Facebook.com/HarlequinBooks

 Twitter.com/HarlequinBooks

 Instagram.com/HarlequinBooks

 Pinterest.com/HarlequinBooks

ReaderService.com

**ROMANCE WHEN
YOU NEED IT**

HFGENRE2017R